The Road to Floradixie

By Tom Brewster

For information, or to order additional
copies, please contact:

Beacon Publishing Group
P.O. Box 41573 Charleston, S.C. 29423
800.817.8480| beaconpublishinggroup.com

Publisher's catalog available by request.

ISBN-13: 978-1-949472-20-2

ISBN-10: 1-949472-20-2

Published in 2020. New York, NY 10001.

First Edition. Printed in the USA.

Chapter One

In 2003 Anderson Claypool was still grieving; still devastated by a crime perpetrated upon a nation and upon him personally. Two years had failed to lessen the pain, and he suspected the ache would always remain if not intensify, but he had found something that temporarily left him feeling avenged.

He watched the bulldozers moving through heaps of concrete and steel, the dust rose into the air, removing the ruin left behind by something so horrendous it was beyond comprehension. He tried not to think past the moment; avoiding memories that were impossible to extinguish. Although what he was doings would have been unthinkable just three years ago, he felt relief in the undertaking.

In 2001 New York City was as foreign to him as the face of the moon, but he studied everything about it, and had become familiar with the things he needed to know. He memorized the subways and path trains crisscrossing the underbelly of the city. It was a simple task, but blending in was a little more difficult, but essential. He was an imposing six feet six inches tall, two hundred and thirty pounds, and black. He was quiet and mysterious. To some people that was scary.

Using a cell phone with all its features, GPS and MapQuest, were totally off limits. Leaving records

1

behind, even in the ether, was unacceptable. He studied the city, all five boroughs. He knew how to escape New York in any direction, but it was imperative not to leave a trace..

Looking for a diversion from the horror of that dreadful day in September 2001 didn't start in the moment and it wouldn't end in a moment, but evening the score was an easement from the dread, and those moments came from revenge.

Sunlight fanned out across the crown of the Statute of Liberty in an emblazoned golden haze at sunset. The last tour to see her in all her glory ended at 5:30 p.m., and the details of the excursion lingered in his mind. He had taken the ferry to Ellis Island and then on to Liberty Island. He shadowed four men who tried in vain to blend in but their facial expressions were grim, tight and besot with anxiety. They studied every detail of the monument, the ferry, and boat traffic in Upper New York Bay, and even the air traffic above. They would have been suspicious even to the untrained eye, but political correctness was so oppressive that a distrustful glance at young Arab men was frowned upon by the enlightened citizenry of New York.

Anderson wasn't suspicious of them - of their intentions. He was past suspicion, he already knew they were up to no good. This was a dry run, practice for treachery. Tomorrow they intended to take the ferry and when they were docked on Liberty Island they would release hellfire onto innocent victims. Two co-conspirators would arrive on Liberty Island in a Super Stock Evinrude with an arsenal of automatic weapons and explosives. Together they would kill every tourist there and bring down the Statute in a firestorm that would circle the globe. They would all die in the process. All for the glory of Allah. It was an unsophisticated plan, but so was bringing down the World Trade Center. If being cremated alive wasn't a deterrent any plan, even one lacking imagination would work as good as any.

They disembarked the ferry at Battery Park and walked a considerable distance to a red brick apartment house in Greenwich Village across from the Cafe Wha. Anderson left them there and made his way to Ground Zero where he grieved again, as he did every single day, scrutinizing the total devastation. Incrementally the rubble was being shoved into heaps as the hole deepened; the ashes of the dead left in the dirt to be dispensed of along with the concrete dust and steel of the World Trade Center. Everything Anderson lived for was blended in the debris leaving him as hollow as the dark empty hole in the ground.

A slight framed elderly woman approached him while he watched the construction activity that would continue on into the night. She placed her hand on his back. He didn't look at her. He didn't want to look at anyone. The pain in his heart was etched in the lines on his face, and he knew she could see it. She carried the same feelings herself.

"Anderson, we've left a package for you in your hotel room," she said. She ran her hand across his back in a consolatory manner.

"I thought we weren't using names," he mumbled.

She ignored the remark. "Good luck, Anderson." she said. The conversation was short. Everything they needed to say had been said a long time ago. She walked back to a car waiting at the curb.

"I'll see you in Memphis, Thelma," calling her by name, forgoing his own admonition. When this was finished, they would be working together as they had been for the last year. He was thankful for Thelma. She was his most trusted ally.

At 3:00 a.m. Anderson opened his eyes, the curtain was pulled back and the light from the illuminated Empire State building radiated into his room. He was at the Double Tree Hotel, located at 120 Ninth St. He washed his face and dressed quickly. He opened the canvas bag to examine the Heckler MP5 machine gun Thelma had provided. He attached the silencer and locked in a 40 round clip. He placed it back into the bag and slung the strap over his shoulder. He took the stairs from the fifth floor to the lobby. A young black woman was sitting in a chair behind the desk. There was hardly room enough behind the counter for a full grown adult to turn around. The lobby was no bigger than an elementary school coat room. The tiny room where he had slept was four hundred dollars per night. Cheap by NYC standards.

"I'm checking out, Miss, but I need to ask a question. I stupidly left my suitcase in the hallway last evening, and when I remembered it this morning, it was gone. I'm hoping someone turned it in here at the desk." Anderson said.

The clerk looked blankly at him. "There's nothing here," she said.

"I hope you have a surveillance system." Anderson said.

She raised her fingertips to her lip nervously. " We do but there was a guy here from the security company just after the manager left yesterday evening. He said there was a problem with the system and he took the recorder and the recordings for the past week. He said he would be back this morning."

That was all Anderson needed to hear. It was confirmation that his face wouldn't be plastered all over the surveillance recordings. His support team members were bonafide professionals. Their names were a mystery, but he knew their work to be superb. He was ninety-nine percent sure they had his back but hearing from the clerk firsthand erased that one percent of doubt. The security video records had been cleaned as promised.

Thirty-five minutes later Anderson emerged from the alley behind Cafe Wha. There were a few people still lingering on the corner of Macdougal Street and Minetta Lane. Anderson quietly moved past them. The vanilla glow from the city lights glistened on the damp brick streets. He stepped off the curb and crossed over to the apartment building. The key he had been provided along with the MP5 was new. Sometimes new keys were difficult but it slipped smoothly into the lock and within seconds he was inside. There was a red door thirteen treads to the top of the stairs, just as he had been told. He moved quickly two steps at a time and when he topped the stairs he kicked the door sending it crashing into the room. It was a bleak, dirty apartment with military grade rifles lying haphazardly on the floor and coffee table. One young man who had been sleeping on the couch and another on the floor on a blow-up mattress snapped awake. They were scrambling, wide-eyed, trying to get to their feet. The flash from the Hecker lit up the room as Anderson put a bullet into the first man's chest, and then the other. He fired two more rounds into each of their heads.

Two men came rushing down the hallway with assault rifles at ready. Their eyes searching frantically through the blue smoke, their expressions laced with fear . Anderson sprayed a battery of hot lead dropping them instantly. A third man had been advancing at him from behind them, but he turned to run. Anderson shot him in the back, and then a final bullet to the head. Five men were down with one left to go. It was quiet and dark. Anderson could hear his own breath in rapid cadence, feel his pulse throbbing in his neck. He slid against the hallway wall until he reached the bedroom door. His eyes bulged, all five senses on high alert as he entered into the dark room, searching for the sixth man. There wasn't a movement, or a sound. It was a small room with a single bed without a lot of room to hide. Anderson opened the closet door and sent a salvo of nine millimeter lead ripping through the clothing, tearing into the plaster wall. A curtain of wallboard dust exploded into the air to permeate the room. His eyes darted about, penetrating the haze looking for the slightest movement. It was as quiet as death itself. With one hand Anderson reached down and grasped the bed railing and spun the bed across the room. A youthful Arab man, a kid really, lie terrified with his hands covering his face. "Don't kill me," he pleaded. Anderson grabbed him by the ankle and dragged him to the center of the room. "Don't kill me," he said again in a whimper, trembling like a beaten dog. He wasn't quite ready for his soul to pass over into the afterlife, not even for the glory of Allah. Anderson lowered the gun and pulled the trigger. It clicked rapidly. The gun was empty. The man's eyes widened and a terrified squeal erupted from his throat. It was short lived - silenced as Anderson sprang upon him and wrapped his hands around his throat. His grip was like a steel vice snapping around the man's neck. He cursed as he squeezed! His fingers ached as he tightened his grip - tighter and tighter until he knew he had murdered him. When he released his grip a death rattle issued quietly from the deceased in abiding surrender.

When it was done Anderson felt better. There were six less terrorist in the world. He exited the front door and walked casually down the sidewalk seemingly as unconcerned about the dead bodies as a mortician after a routine day at the office, but inside he was raging, white hot with emotion.

.And then from a darkened alley a squad car approached him and slowly rolled to a stop. A young policeman got out and walked towards him. Anderson was calm, but he realized things could go south in a hurry. He was confident he could fight his way out of any situation, but he had decided early on that he was never going to kill a cop. His options were to wait to see what developed. If things went badly he would try to disarm the policeman, or last ditch option, run. He didn't have to think about it long, in just a moment his anxiety was put to bed.

The cop advanced towards him. "Anderson," he said softly.

Anderson eyes narrowed like an eagle accessing his prey. From the tone of the cop's voice he was hopeful but not quite ready to believe he was in the clear. In the fog of war death might come from anywhere but help also came from unexpected forces.

"There's a car waiting around the corner," the cop said.

Anderson's brow furrowed. "Where is it taking me?

"To a safe place."

Anderson paused for a long moment; What's this to you?

"My dad was in the World Trade Center when it came down," he said.

Anderson watched as the cop walked back to his car. "I thought we weren't using names," Anderson said.

The cop smiled."Thank you, Anderson, for your service to our country," he said.

Chapter Two

In Willoughby Hills, Illinois, seven years later and a universe away from New York City, not in distance, but in culture and attitudes, life was about to change for two old cops marking time in retirement.

It was 7:45 a.m. and scorching hot. Sweat poured down Morgan Cooper's back leaving sweaty blotches on his shirt. A sharp pain from the tendon in his wrist shot up his arm. He changed hands then continued pumping gas and groaned while rubbing his elbow. At that moment his thoughts were interrupted.

"Morgan, what's happen'n, old boy?" a booming voice came from behind him. It was Rudy Campbell, Morgan's lifelong friend. They had been on the Willoughby Hills Police Department together for most of Morgan's 28-year tenure. Now they were both retired. Morgan loved Rudy like a brother, but he could put his teeth on edge quicker than anyone he knew.

"Why ya hold'n your elbow like that, Morgan?" Rudy bellowed.

"Rudy, I'm not across the street, I'm right next to you!" Morgan said.

Rudy's hearing headed south during the eighties but he stayed on patrol missing radio calls that he couldn't hear until the mid-nineties. One night Rudy was reported to be driving slowly behind the

9

Willoughby Hills Park District shining his spotlight at a hoot owl roosting in a tree while his fellow officers responded to an armed robbery call. At that point his career promptly came to an end. After a brief investigation he was deemed to be unfit for duty. He had twenty-six years under his belt so the department simply retired his badge under honorable conditions, putting him out to pasture. Nowadays Rudy drew his retirement, hung around Freda's Restaurant drinking free coffee with active duty policemen, trying to hold onto the past. He shouted his way through the day because he couldn't hear himself talking, but stubbornly refused to use a hearing aid.

"Morgan, why ya busting your butt serving them papers?" Rudy said, flipping the end of Morgan's necktie, a sly smile across his round face.

"Rudy, I know you're deaf, but I've told you enough times now that I know you've heard me at least once. My retirement's gone - wasted on a foolish endeavor. I have to work for a living!"

Morgan rolled his retirement over into stocks during the nineties and lost most of it. The captain's son, fresh out of college, talked him into a "fail-safe" mutual fund and over the years it went the way of sand through his fingers. Early on he liked Enron and General Motors, but his coup de gras was AIG.

Morgan took the Illinois Private Detective test and acquired a license a year after leaving the Department. There wasn't much money in private investigations but under the Private Detective Act he could serve legal documents like the sheriff's deputies. It paid well, but it was boring and tedious. Recently serving process had become a full-time occupation.

Rudy took the test four times and flunked it. Now he harassed Morgan about being a glorified process server. It was purely a case of unmitigated jealousy.

Morgan headed across the gas station service drive to pay for his gas. His foot was aching so he fetched the ibuprofen from his pocket.

"Why ya limping like that, Morgan?" Rudy shouted.

"I've got tendonitis in my heel. It usually last a couple of days."

"It's hell to be old and fat, ain't it, Morgan?

Morgan was ten pounds heavier than he was when he joined the police department. Rudy was forty over and gaining.

"At least I can get my shirt buttoned," Morgan said, pointing to an opening in Rudy's shirt seam where a hairy patch of belly was trying to force its way out.

"I might be fat, but can you do this?" he roared. He jumped into the air, clicked his heels together, tapped his toes on the concrete, then spun in a circle, laughing the entire time.

Two little girls in a car on the service drive giggled at his antics.

"I gotta get a cup of coffee and get going," Morgan said.

Rudy followed him inside. "You know how to tell when you're gett'n old, don't ya, Morgan?"

Morgan stared at him indifferently.

"You've finished washing your hair before you're done peeing!" he cackled.

Several patrons turned to look at him. Morgan exhaled and shook his head.

"Morgan, I need to talk to you about something

important," he said, quickly becoming serious.

"Rudy, I'm in a hurry. I have to go to Beardstown to serve a summons. Maybe later," he said, cutting him off.

Rudy stared at Morgan. He was annoyed by Morgan's stolidity. He had known Morgan all his life. They were in the same high school graduating class, played high school baseball together. They were both mediocre athletes, but Morgan was always just a little bit better. Morgan batted seventh in the lineup on the baseball team, Rudy ninth. Neither of them were honors graduates but Morgan was ranked a little higher in class standings. Morgan's parents were elementary school teachers, and Rudy's dad was the custodian at the high school. They took the police exam together and Morgan finished third on the eligibility list. Rudy was thirteenth. They had a lot in common but Morgan thought he was just a little bit better than Rudy, in Rudy's opinion. But still they were best friends, in spite of Rudy's envy.

"Morgan, we gotta talk now," Rudy grumbled, irritated by Morgan's indifference. He retrieved a folded piece of paper from his back pocket, wet with sweat. He fanned it in the air. Morgan could see it was a wanted poster he had taken from the break room at the police station. Retired personnel were not allowed in the squad rooms, but they were welcome in the break room. Rudy spent a good part of his day there pestering cops and drinking free coffee.

Morgan snorted in disbelief, stepped into his car and started to close the door.

"You're an asshole, Morgan! You think you're so smart because you passed the Private Detective test, and you're soooo good because you left the department with a pat on the back and a gold watch while I got retired for being hard of hear'n. You're soooo good 'cause you didn't get as fat as me, and you get to run all over the country serving papers!"

Rudy stopped and searched the recesses of his mind for something to say to buttress his plea. Anything would do! "Well, I know you're still mad because you struck out in the ninth inning at the regionals with the tying run on third, and I drove him in with a sac fly!" Rudy barked, referring to a time so far back that it couldn't actually be recalled. It was insignificant but it had become a frequently referenced event between them. Now Rudy was using it to muddle the issue.

" That again? Thirty-five years ago, give me a break, Rudy!"

Rudy's chest heaved., sweat poured from his thick salt and pepper hair and streamed down his face. Rudy had an Irish name but his features were clearly Italian. His face was round as a dinner plate, dark clear skin set off by intense black eyes, and a nose that could have had Corgliano written on it, that being his mother's maiden name. He wiped the sweat off his face, pushing it back into his hair line, calmer now. He thought for a moment about his rant.

"Well, at least I got the hair," he smirked. His remarks about baseball and his hair were clearly unrelated to anything relevant, but somehow Rudy thought his inane comparisons were leveling the playing field.

"Get your fat butt in the car. You can go with me, you got nothing else to do." Morgan said, half smiling, giving in to his old buddy. "And besides that, it was a foul ball and the right fielder should have let it drop," Morgan said, making a faint attempt dispute Rudy's claim.

Beardstown was 28 miles from Willoughby Hills. Morgan drove while Rudy talked. The wanted poster he so urgently wanted Morgan to see was a bulletin on one Jose Garcia, a burglary suspect who had fled Memphis, Tennessee. He had been last seen in Hollywood, Florida and Rudy wanted to go get him. It was just the latest of Rudy's never ending pipe dreams.

In the beginning of the conversation Rudy adamantly professed to have inside information on Jose Garcia but Morgan wasn't convinced. Every city and town in America with an Hispanic population had at least five men with that name, real or assumed. Before the conversation was over and facts were examined, Rudy didn't actually have the inside skinny on Garcia; but rather Rudy's daughter taught English classes in a vocational school for Spanish-speaking students in Memphis. He had questioned her at length assuming that she had detailed knowledge of every Hispanic person in the city. Amazingly, she had heard rumors due to a generous reward for Garcia's apprehension. That was enough to send Rudy over the edge.

Why Rudy would concern himself with it in the first place was absurd, but that was vintage Rudy. He didn't display the same curiosity when he was actually a police officer, but in his retirement he couldn't think about anything but crime. His congressman's telephone number was on his speed dial and the Department of Homeland Security knew him by name. He was on the phone shouting about something to someone in authority on a daily basis. He knew every face on every wanted poster in the break room and was determined to bring in a dangerous wanted criminal in his waning years.

Rudy wasn't much different than most new age Americans. Old actors and actresses continued to take parts in movies as characters they were too old to play, baseball players tried to play beyond their years, and people in all walks of life worked out in fit clubs trying to stay young. There was a day when American presidents left office and quietly went away, or died in office like Franklin Roosevelt, or retired and did something absurd like LBJ sporting a shoulder length ponytail in obscurity. In 2009 Jimmy Carter was still trying to interfere in foreign affairs, and Bill Clinton was off to North Korea to free a captive journalist. The world was a different place now.

Morgan liked things as they were in the old days. Policemen retired to their front porches to drink coffee, drank beer at fraternal organization bars and eagerly anticipated spring when they could break out their fishing gear. They didn't research every new law regarding national security or scrutinize every wanted poster in the break room. They didn't lose their retirements in the stock market because regular uninformed people didn't get into the stock market, and they didn't risk their life savings on things they knew nothing about.

Listening to Rudy's wild scheme was unavoidable now that they were in the car together, and Rudy was routing him into a direction he didn't want to go.

Rudy knew the burglary victim in Memphis

was very well-to-do, angry, and he was offering a reward for information about Jose Garcia. This guy would pay anything to see that no good low life brought to justice, according to Rudy.

Morgan wasn't convinced, but even more perturbing to Rudy was that Morgan didn't care. He wasn't interested in catching criminals. He wasn't interested in anything. Paying his bills, serving papers and waiting to die was Morgan's lot in life.

Before October 2007, Morgan was the most fascinating person Rudy knew. He was one of those people who attracted interest wherever he went. He was well-informed on most issues, well-spoken, good-looking and in great physical condition. Women were attracted to him, but he never encouraged them. Why would he? He was married to the love of his life, but now things were different. Morgan had not smiled a real smile since October 12th, 2007. That was the day Molly died. Morgan was 62 years old and his life was over. It concerned Rudy that his interest had waned and getting him involved in anything was like pulling teeth.

Still, Rudy continued to ramble. He wanted Morgan to take a few weeks off and go with him to Memphis to follow up on the Jose Garcia scheme. Since Morgan was an Illinois licensed Private Detective, authorized to do investigations, it was his civic duty to do the investigation, according to Rudy. Garcia was, after all, an illegal immigrant.

"Who said he was illegal?" Morgan asked.

"The wanted poster!"

According to Rudy, the flood of people from Mexico and South America wasn't immigration but more of an invasion. They wanted to change our flag, adulterate our language and undo our way of life. And now think of the unmitigated gall of Jose Garcia, sneaking into our country and burglarizing one of our rich angry citizens in Memphis, Tennessee. It was too much to bear. He was going after him!

Morgan questioned Rudy as to how they would implement such a plan. Would they simply locate the victim's address, drive up to the house and introduce themselves as the answer to his problem?

"Okay, Mr. Burglary Victim, we're a couple of retired policemen from Willoughby Hills, Illinois, a burgeoning metropolis of 30,000 people (31,000, Rudy interrupted,) without benefit of either of us having been promoted to detective while we were actually on the police department, and we're here to bring Mr. Jose Garcia to justice," Morgan said facetiously.

"Morgan, you should have made detective ten years ago, but we only had two dicks and those hard heads wouldn't retire. They filled up the position until we were too old to get the job! Besides that you're a full-fledged detective now."

"Glorified process server, didn't you just say?"

As crazy as the idea was, Morgan promised to think about it. That night Morgan lay in bed listening to the crickets outside the balcony. It was still hot, but both of the double doors were open. A breeze was flowing through the room, and the outside noises filtered in. Morgan loved that balcony in spite of the way he argued with Molly against putting it in. It was now one of his greatest pleasures. Molly was so determined to have those French doors and the balcony overlooking her fountain and flower garden that she banged a hole in the wall with a sledgehammer while he was on duty. He had the choice of fixing the wall or giving in to her. He did as he usually did when she wanted something. He built a balcony with French doors.

Morgan slipped out of bed and walked out onto the balcony. He did the same thing every night before he went to sleep. He looked down over the flagstone walk, lined with impatients and hostas and solar lights. The groundcover she installed the first year they lived there was inching its way over the walkway. He knew it was time to trim it back. He couldn't let it get into Molly's fountain. She told him that it had a tendency to work its way into the receptacle where it would clog up the pump. The garden contained black-eyed susans, his personal favorite flower, wild Queen Ann's Lace, his mother's weed of choice, and various red and green ornamental grasses, mixed in with the variety of more domestic Asian and dramatic canna lilies. Molly had asked him what his favorite flowers were because she wanted him to enjoy her garden as much as she did. He remembered his mother told him that when she was a little girl she would lie in a field of Queen Ann's Lace, dotted with black eyed susans as she watch the clouds floating across the sky. In lieu of actually knowing any other flower by name he thought that was his best uninformed answer.

Black Eyed Susans were easy to come by at the local nursery, but she had to drive to the country to find the Queen Ann's Lace growing wild. Molly didn't know that the first time he realized the weed with those white doilies bobbing in the wind alongside the road as Queen Ann's Lace was the day she planted it in the garden. He thought they were gracefully beautiful, and now he could put a name to them.

He watched the water flowing over the top of the vase, splashing onto the field rocks around it, finding its way back to the tank beneath the ground. He could almost see Molly sitting in the glow of the muted fountain light in her white night gown with her head tilted back gazing at the stars. He missed her more now than he did when she said goodbye.

He went back to his bed and closed his eyes. He thought if he could just go to sleep and never wake up, fear would not interfere with his passing. If he could just vanish into the abyss sometime during the night he wouldn't have to reckon with the reality of dying. He just didn't want to "be" anymore. As usual, he drifted away.

At 2:30 a.m., Morgan opened his eyes. I'm still alive, he thought. He reached across to the lamp table and retrieved his cell phone. He hit #1 and pressed the send button. After a few rings Rudy picked up the phone.

"What's wrong?" he shouted.

"I'm in," Morgan said.

Chapter Three

It took a week, but the day came when Morgan and Rudy set out along the highway headed into what was certainly nothing less than foolishness. He and Molly had been on vacation several times with Rudy throughout the years, along with Rudy's first and second wives, so traveling with Rudy wasn't anything new.

Knowing Rudy's track record, Molly refused to have a relationship with his third wife so she wisely chose not to get too comfortable with her. They skipped a few years of vacations with him, and inevitably the third wife went hiking and found her way to her daughter's house where she texted Rudy of her intention to take up permanent residency there or anywhere away from him. Molly was sick the following year and vacations with Rudy were in the past.

Now they were off on another trip, but it wasn't a vacation. It was no more than folly, but Morgan had decided in the middle of the night that his life was totally meaningless as it was. Taking a trip with Rudy would at least be a diversion. He was tired of eating his dinner standing at the kitchen sink staring out the window watching his neighbor's dog barking at every movement. His heart couldn't take another evening of sitting at the dining room table looking at the computer slide show of Molly digging in the flower garden or squirting a garden hose at the camera. He obviously wasn't going to die in his sleep as he prayed for, so he was all in. Anything had to be better than lying in the dark staring at the ceiling. Now he and Rudy were going after that no good Jose Garcia! At least it would be a different kind of misery.

Memphis, Tennessee is most famous for Elvis Presley and Beale Street. It's likely if you're there you'll see both. Downtown Memphis has a steady flow of tourist and local music lovers parading through the city streets heading towards Beale. It was hard to imagine a corner without a "bad" Elvis whose only resemblance to the King is a white spangled jumpsuit. Morgan had been there during the eighties but hadn't been back since. Now they were en route to find a rich, bitter, burglary victim, although Rudy's focus was hitting the bars on Beale Street.

Silky O'Sullivan's was Rudy's preferred destination, with the dueling piano players, local singers, and accommodations honed to rustic perfection. Outside the beer garden hopped with live music as goats meandered up and down a heavy wooden spiral staircase at their leisure. An oddity to people outside Memphis, but locals were used to seeing goats there as well as the parade of ducks in the fountain at the four star Peabody Hotel.

Rudy loved music and he got down with it. He didn't love it in the same way Morgan loved it, but he had a passion. For Morgan, music could tell a whole life story in a song. There weren't enough words in the English language to express the emotion a good song could extract from Morgan's bewildered soul.

As for Rudy, it was something in the beat that worked its way inside him and caused him to and sway like a big ship on a wave. Sometimes he had difficulty hearing it and it didn't matter that he looked like a man with his pants full of fire ants. One of his most endearing and at the same time most frustrating traits was that he simply could not be embarrassed. The songs he liked made him happy, something the casual observer couldn't resist about him. He didn't worry about making a fool of himself nor was he aware of his tone-deafness.

They arrived as the sun was setting behind the empty hulking Pyramid on the banks of the Mississippi River, the largest structure of its kind in the western world, the former home of the Memphis Grizzles, now abandoned and empty. In a short time they were in Memphis strolling down Union Street past the Peabody Hotel. Live music called out into the night from Beale Street and hung out in the air heavy with humidity and stale beer. A hard steel kind of blues jangled into the streets from Rum Boogie's, rock n roll banged off the walls at Alfred's, and sweet soul poured out of BB King's. W.C. Handy's bronze statue leaned forward at 4th and Beale, as if watching tourist with yellow wristbands drinking "Big Ass Beers" from plastic cups. Beale Street was jammed.

They were checked for identification at the corner of Broadway and Beale before they were allowed past the barricades. Rudy cackled. He hadn't been carded since he was nineteen years old. Morgan snorted at the security guard indignantly.

"That's ridiculous. I'm sixty two years old!"

"Rules are that we check everybody, dude. Move it on."

Morgan and Rudy carefully avoided tourist who banged into each other, spilling beer as they swayed with the music. People were lined up in cubbyholes between buildings listening to bands on make-shift platforms at the ends of alleyways. Every amateur in Tennessee wanted a gig on Beale Street and even a barrel stand in an alley was a highly sought after location. Every age and social status was there milling about, curiously looking each other over and talking too loudly.

"What are we doing here?" Morgan said, as much to himself as to Rudy.

"A little rest and relaxation before doing the heavy lift'n, Morgan, old boy." Rudy said.

Morgan rolled his eyes.

He saw beautiful women in skimpy clothing hanging onto their boyfriends and lovers deeply immersed in each other. He ached inside as he watched it blossom. It was like being on the sidelines without having any hope of ever being involved. It was a pain so deep that it simply consumed him. There was nothing left unaffected. His body hurt, and inside his mind he agonized. He saw Molly in every woman's face and it made him want to run away and vanish buried within himself. Still he walked quietly beside Rudy without an outward sign of the inside turmoil.

They stopped on the sidewalk and watched the goats with their heads stuck through the spindles on the staircase studying the crowd as though curious about such bizarre behavior. Morgan and Rudy inched along with the crowd towards the main entrance. Rudy fished inside his pocket for his badge and had it ready at the door. He barged past the security guard, flipped his badge, pointed his thumb over his shoulder and said, "He's with me."

"Ho'd on, ho'd on," the security guard said as he reigned Rudy back to the doorway.

"Silky never charges cops," Rudy said defiantly. Mere speculation, but right on the mark.

"You got tat right, but I gotta be shore you's da real deal."

Rudy held his badge at eye level while the guard examined it.

"Retired?"

"Twenty six years of fight'n crime," Rudy stated proudly.

The guard eyeballed their gray hair and glanced at Rudy's bulging belly.

"Go on ahead then, but don't be hurtin yourself in there," he said.

Rudy hopped up, clicked his heels and gave him a head nod. The guard giggled like a child. He slapped Rudy's back and pushed him along.

Silky's was jumping. The pianos were quietly playing as one of the piano players coaxed a newlywed couple onto the stage.

"Where you'all from?" he asked as he extended a hand to the bride assisting her onto the platform.

"Jonesboro, Arkansas," the groom answered.

"Then this would be your sister?"

The bar crowd roared.

"No, the bride screeched as she tried to step down from the stage in retreat.

The piano player tightened his grasp. "Just an old

Arkansas joke, baby," he said.

The groom laughed and received the first of a lifetime of scornful glances from his new bride. The crowd roared again.

Rudy gouged Morgan in the ribs with his elbow. "Get it, Morgan?"

"No, Rudy, help me out," Morgan said sarcastically.

"They're newlyweds, and when the groom said, Jonesbo------."

"Rudy, I get it!"

Rudy shoved his way up to the bar and came back with two mugs of beer. They stood around for awhile until a pedestal-like table was vacated by a middle-aged couple.

Morgan sipped his beer and watched Rudy skip from one table to another robustly imparting his wisdom. Most people thought he was merely trying to be heard over the music, unbeknownst to them that was his normal conversational tone. Still, as usual, everybody welcomed him and wanted him in their crowd. How could he be so oblivious to every social rule in the books and still be the guy everybody wanted to be around!

At one point he saw Rudy corner the door security guard who was on his way to the men's room. He had pulled the wanted poster out of his pocket and was poking it with his big round finger while the guard uncomfortably and unsuccessfully tried to escape Rudy on his terms. When he returned to the table he said, "I've got the skinny on this burglary victim, so we can relax now."

He looked relaxed already, Morgan thought.

Rudy was resting his elbows on the table,

spilled beer soaking his forearms. Two Arab gentlemen were attempting to get through the crowd when they finally came to Rudy. The first was middle-aged and the other in his twenties. The first man said, "Excuse, please," three times but Rudy had his back to him and didn't hear. Morgan touched Rudy's shoulder and pointed to the men who were waiting patiently. Rudy turned and looked at them blankly.

"Excuse, please."

"Oh, sure!" Rudy said, moving quickly aside.

Both men smiled and nodded thank you.

"But don't go off bombing anybody," Rudy cackled. "You know, boom, boom."

The older man continued to smile but the younger man's eyes narrowed and he glared at Rudy. He leaned over and whispered to the other man, explaining the connotation. His eyes narrowed as anger swept across his face.

"Fuk on you!" he snorted.

The younger man stepped by staring at Rudy until he was glaring over his shoulder. "Fuk on yourself!" he said as he disappeared into the crowd.

"What got into them?" Rudy asked.

Morgan gave Rudy a pathetic glance.

As the evening progressed, Rudy downed beer like it was water, and Morgan sipped. It was almost 1:00 a.m., when the pianos were ringing out Blue Suede Shoes. Rudy was on the stage with a mic in hand doing his best Elvis impression. One player was pounding on the keyboard, but the other was up dancing around Rudy clapping his hands and laughing. Was it possible that Rudy was actually that entertaining?"

A beautiful dark-haired woman with large

round eyes had been watching Morgan for most of the last hour. He noticed her, but just the thought of looking at any woman who wasn't Molly left him with a sick feeling. When she stopped at his table and started a conversation, Morgan was immediately nervous. At sixty-two, he still looked like a bashful little boy. Many women can't resist that, and along with the alcohol stoking her imagination, she was an immediate admirer. She was quick to sit down in Rudy's vacant seat. Morgan noticed a feral lust when her skirt flashed open and exposed her thighs. He held his breath, immediately suppressing his arousal.

He tried not to be impolite, but after a short time he excused himself and went to the exit. The security guard asked if he had enough fun for the day?"

"I guess," Morgan said.

"Well, be careful out there. They's some real mean crap goin down on them streets this time-a night."

"I will. Thanks."

Morgan walked south to Anchor Street and sat down on the curb. Tears welled in his eyes. "Molly, Molly, Molly."

Rudy was panicked. "Where are ya, Morgan?" he whispered to himself as he hurried to the door and looked outside. The security guard pointed his thumb south.

"He went thatta away."

Rudy hurried south, noticing the crowd had waned. He looked for Morgan and shouted. Morgan raised his hand and Rudy was relieved.

"What the hell you doin' down here, Morgan?"

Morgan looked up and Rudy saw the tears. He

exhaled and stared with empathy. "What am I gonna do with you, Morgan?" Rudy said as he clumsily lowered himself onto the concrete. "I saw a beautiful woman hitt'n on you in there, and then the next minute you was gone."

Morgan was quiet for several minutes, but finally he spoke. "Do you remember Anita Crawford, Rudy?" he asked quietly.

Rudy nodded.

"Well, Anita married Bobby Crowe right after high school. He was drafted before the ink was dry on the marriage license. Three months later he was dead - killed in Vietnam."

"I liked old Bobby," Rudy said.

"I didn't see Anita for about two years after that. When I did, one thing led to another. We started dating, and after awhile we got sort of serious. Anita loved sex. She was affectionate you know, real sweet, very involved sexually. Anyway the thing was – she cried just a little every time she had a climax. It didn't last long, just a short whimper. Sometimes it was so quiet you could barely hear it, but she always cried. I asked her about it but she never answered. I never asked her again. We weren't in love, and when I met Molly, it was all over. One look at Molly and I never wanted anybody else."

The thing is that I was always curious about why she cried. Tonight I learned the reason." He tightened his lips and exhaled. "That woman who stopped at our table was beautiful. When she sat down she opened her legs and I saw her thighs. Rudy, I wanted her. Just for a split second I wanted her."

Rudy watched Morgan in anticipation, but

Morgan stopped there. Rudy grimaced.

"I wanted her too, and I didn't even see her thighs, Morgan. But what's that got to do with Anita Crawford?"

"Anita cried every time she climaxed - every single time." Morgan ran his hands through his hair. "Rudy, she cried because I wasn't Bobby."

Rudy studied Morgan for a long moment then said, "Well, old Anita could have been like you, Morgan. She could have withered away and died without another minute of happiness, but she didn't. She found somebody to make love to her, even if it did make her cry."

Morgan wasn't insulted. Strangely he admired Rudy for his straight-forwardness. He knew too that Rudy wasn't finished. He waited for the rest of it.

"Morgan, do ya think Molly would have wanted this for you? I mean, sitt'n in a gutter bawling your eyes out. I knew Molly. She didn't want this for you. She asked me before she died to take care of you. I promised her I would. I would have tried anyway, but I promised her. That sealed the deal. That's what she wanted. Do you think she would have asked the dummest, fun-lovinest fool she ever knew to take care of you if she didn't want you to go on with your life?"

Morgan stared at Rudy. He did actually have a big dumb look on his face - a comical yet strange expression. At first Morgan smiled, then he chuckled. Finally he laughed out loud. The tears were rolling down his cheeks but he couldn't stop laughing. Rudy laughed too. He flopped back on the concrete and covered his eyes with his forearm and roared.

"You fat (more laughter), you fat..." Tears

were dropping off Morgan's cheeks.

"You fat fun-lov'n fool!" Morgan cackled uncontrollably. It wasn't even funny but it was as if years of dammed up tension had been released.

After several minutes they both regained control. Morgan was still smiling. It was the first good laugh he had since Molly died and it felt good. He jumped up and gave Rudy a hand. In cadence, they started walking south.

"You gotta stop calling me fat, Morgan. I'm not really that fat. My shirts are just too tight."

"You have to get some new shirts then," Morgan said, eyeballing the patch of belly shining through the buttonhole.

Neither Morgan nor Rudy were paying attention as they walked, but it was getting darker. Finally they stopped, realizing they had wandered into a depressed part of town. Rudy glanced around nervously. "There ain't many people left around here. And if you ain't noticed, we're the only white men on the streets."

"That doesn't mean anything, Rudy."

"Means we better head the other direction," Rudy protested.

"You're right, we're going the wrong way," Morgan said, looking at the street sign. The buildings were dark and empty and steel fences enclosed deep holes in the ground where buildings once stood. "There weren't many people on Beale Street either," Morgan added as an afterthought.

"Pale faces anyway," Rudy snorted.

They turned and started in the direction from where they had come, but at that instant they saw two black men hurrying across the street where they stepped into a doorway. It looked suspicious, but they weren't going to panic. Morgan led the way and they crossed the street. The two men crossed the street ahead of them in an obvious attempt to keep pace with them. Rudy dropped down on one knee and retrieved a 380 automatic from his ankle holster. He picked a zap from his back pocket and handed it to Morgan. He pushed the gun into his waistband.

"You brought a gun," Morgan said, stating the obvious.

"Thanks to George Bush, retired cops can carry." Rudy answered.

Morgan wasn't armed. He knew there were new laws allowing retired cops to possess guns, and cross state lines with them, but he didn't believe he would ever need one. He was happy to see that Rudy wasn't as naive

"Don't use it unless you have to," Morgan urged.

Morgan's heart was beating in his ear, his breath was growing more rapid. He was calm on the surface, but he knew his heart rate was racing. They were just small town cops, but both of them had been in many dangerous situations over the years, but many years had passed since then, and now they were both way over the hill. At a disadvantage, to say the least.

As they advanced Morgan stepped off the sidewalk to cross the street again, and Rudy followed a few steps behind. Just then a third man emerged. Slim, white guy, about 5'10'', wearing a wife beater t-shirt, his body shadowed in tattoos.

"Feel better, Rudy? He's white."

Morgan stopped and waited as Rudy hurried to catch up.

"Where ya go'n fat boy?" the wife-beater yelled.

Rudy kept walking. Wife-beater ran into the street cutting them off. The other two black men followed a few feet behind him.

"I said, where ya go'n, fat boy?"

His oily hair was matted to his head, and his skin pale. Some of his tattoos were childlike, probably homemade. He smacked of pimping and pushing drugs, but even a sleazeball like that occasionally fell on hard times and had to roll a tourist to make ends meet. Morgan knew his name. It was Loser. A parasite like that was the same in Tennessee as in Willoughby Hills. Suddenly Morgan wasn't 62 anymore. He was a young tough cop assessing a situation. Rudy sensed it and his confidence gathered steam.

Loser twirled a straight razor, slicing the air. One of the black men had a piece of pipe and the other stood with fist clenched.

"I need yer wallet, Grandpa," he said.

Rudy looked him straight in the eye. The parasite saw Rudy's stare. He knew instantly that this wasn't going the way he wanted.

"Is that all ya got?" Rudy snarled.

"It's good enough to hand you your ass," he said.

Rudy picked the .380 from his waistband in a practiced movement and leveled it at the parasite's head. "I don't think so," he shouted.

Morgan pounced toward the man with the pipe. He had the zap cocked and ready to swing. "I'll bust your head wide open!" he shouted. His eyes were bulging and his lips grimaced into a tight line. The pipe dropped to the ground and went ringing down the street. The third man was gone like a rabbit into the night. Morgan's man had his hands raised over his head in surrender.

The parasite dropped the straight razor. "Okay, go on. It's cool," he said, trying to sound composed.

"Go on my butt," Rudy said, stuffing the .380 back into his belt. "Put up your fist, dirtbag!"

The parasite smirked in disbelief. He backed up a step, then raised his fists. "This must be my lucky day." He danced a Muhammad Ali shuffle, then started to come after Rudy with a right cross. Rudy lunged forward with all 245 pounds landing his meaty fist across the parasite's nose. Blood and snot squirted into the air and Parasite was unfurled on the sidewalk. Rudy stood over him ready to let fly with another shot. The would be thief groaned but he didn't move.

The other man watched with his hands still stretched into the air. Rudy was breathing as though he had just run the 400 meter. "Do we want to take'em in, Morgan, or let 'em go with a warning?"

"I've got a better idea, Rudy," he said as he approached his man. He smacked the zap across his head with a thud. The man went down with a yelp. Blood squirted out of his hairline but he was still conscious. "Get up, empty your pockets!"

The man was quickly on his feet, digging in his pants pockets. He fetched out a dollar and eighteen cents. Morgan snatched it and jammed it into his pants. "Now get over there and empty your buddy's pockets," he ordered

33

Rudy was astonished, but amused.

Parasite moaned as the other man rolled him over digging out singles. "He's got eleven dollars."

"Give it to me," Morgan demanded. He timidly handed the crumpled, dirty one dollar bills to Morgan. Morgan stared at him for a long moment, then raised the zap in an intimidating manner. "Get!" he shouted. The man ran for an alleyway, scurrying like a mouse between two buildings.

As they walked back to Beale Street, Rudy wore a smug little smile, a mix of self- satisfaction and disbelief. He walked and huffed for air, occasionally he glanced at Morgan checking his demeanor. Finally he said, "Man, you went postal."

"It was just a little therapy, Rudy."

It wasn't textbook therapy, but it was therapy that worked. Undoubtedly, the parasite would stick to pimping and roughing up whores, but eventually he would get a shank between his ribs by some fed-up streetwalker.

But tonight it was the Willoughby Hills duo .who did the counseling.

"Was that therapy for him, or you?" Rudy chuckled.

"I have to admit, I liked whacking that zap across his head. And the money? Even a sleazeball like that needs an Egg McMuffin once in awhile, and when he gets hungry, he'll think about us."

Chapter Four

So that was that. Two wandering old retired cops from a little midwest town had blown into the big city with a bang. They danced the dance, sang the songs, and beat two would-be robbers senseless. A finer diversion couldn't have been ordered up to relieve Morgan's tormented soul. In spite of how he tried to hold onto his misery, a good hair-raising scuffle with a couple of gutter dwellers had cobbled over his distress, if only for a moment.

It was confirmation for Rudy. He believed people and things were the same no matter where you found them. A fight for your life was no less intense on the manicured lawn of a suicidal bank executive who was hellbent on leaving the world with a cop as his traveling companion, as it was to wipe the sidewalk with human debris who wanted to rob you and cut you with a straight razor. Cops were cops, and rubbish was rubbish. It didn't matter if it were in Memphis, Tennessee, or back home in Willoughby Hills. He was retired, hard of hearing, and out of his jurisdiction, but by the grace of God, he was still a cop!

They found their way to the Holiday Inn and checked in. Two inebriated young ladies were on their way out wagging their behinds as they sometimes do.

" Gentlemen," they said in unison as they pranced by, smiling and giggling. Rudy held the door and watched their backsides as they strutted onto the street.

"It's just start'n for them, but it's over for us," he said.

"In more ways than one," Morgan agreed.

"Gentlemen," Rudy chuckled, mimicking their sweet young accents. Morgan glanced at him and smiled. "Gentlemen," he repeated. Morgan tried to suppress a laugh in vain. He snorted, and snickered, and finally he belly-laughed. Rudy bellowed and slapped Morgan across his back.

Morgan composed himself, but Rudy was like a little boy who had stumbled upon something funny and he wasn't giving it up. "Gentlemen." Rudy repeated in a high-pitched voice.

"Okay, Rudy, that's enough," Morgan said, but an uncontrollable laughed erupted from inside, and tears rolled down his cheek. He couldn't stop. He was like a little kid in church grappling with a giggling fit.

"That ain't right, you don't have that kind of a laugh in you anymore, Morgan,"

They were both standing in the doorways to their rooms. Morgan unlocked his door, turned to Rudy and smiled. Rudy's door was open but he was waiting like a child for a "good night."

" Fuk on yourself, Rudy. Fuk on you!" Morgan said imitating the Arab man they had seen at Silky's

Rudy smiled and disappeared inside. That was as close as he was going to get to a "good night"

When Morgan was awakened by a knocking at his door, he didn't have any idea where he was. He searched for the light switch on the wall beside his bed for several seconds before he realized that he wasn't at home. It was dark in the room and he was completely disoriented. He got out of bed and found the window curtain and pulled it back. Bright sunlight filled the room assaulting his senses. It looked like it was midday. The knocking continued but seemed more urgent as the seconds passed. Morgan found his way to the door. It was Rudy. He looked fresh and ready to go.

"What are you doin', Morgan? I thought you was dead."

Morgan glanced at his watch. It was 9:45 a.m. "Moses! I haven't slept so hard in years."

Rudy rambled on facetiously about how he feared Morgan had died from the previous evening's trepidation. Simply fell over dead from all the excitement, he thought.

"Good word, Rudy, trepidation."

He was standing in the middle of Morgan's room with a shopping bag bulging with purchases. He had obviously taken Morgan seriously about the new shirts. Morgan suspected that the whore monger calling him "fat boy," may have forced him into it. A scumbag in a wife beater t-shirt disparaging his appearance was downright pestiferous.

His face was glowing like an Arab trader who had cut a deal equivalent to rubbing his opponent's head with his left hand. He emptied the bag onto Morgan's bed and fanned out four Polo shirts. They were red, green, black and maroon.

"I got 'em on sale at Everything Memphis," he said proudly.

They were certainly quality shirts, with a heavy

tightly woven material, and the seams were double stitched.

"How much?" Morgan asked.

"Eleven dollars each," Rudy said. Morgan had closed the bathroom door for privacy, but when Rudy proudly declared the price, Morgan came back out with his toothbrush in his mouth, and toothpaste on his chin. "What?"

"Eleven dollars each."

"No way," Morgan said as he approached the bed to examine the shirts. He picked up the black one and smiled. "Where'd you get these shirts?"

"Everything Memphis, a little shop in Peabody Place."

"Everything Memphis, like the Memphis Zoo?"

"Yeah, like the zoo, the Red Birds, Beale Street., the Grizzles, Mud Island. Everything Memphis"

"Like the Memphis Zoo?"

"Yes, like the Memphis Zoo! Why?"

Morgan ran his finger across the monogram slowly and smiled in a sheepish way. It took Rudy a moment for it to sink in realizing the tiny monogram said Memphis Zoo.

"You bought shirts with a Memphis Zoo logo," he chuckled.

Ruddy picked up the shirts and jammed them into the bag and huffed out of the room.

Later they moseyed down Union St., towards Denny's Restaurant. Morgan didn't have the sensation that they were in hot pursuit of a dangerous criminal who had invaded America, robbed our affluent citizens then fled to Hollywood, Florida. It seemed more like they were on a drinking binge, consisting of crying jags, and spontaneous violent outbreaks. Rudy was wearing his new black Memphis Zoo shirt, and new khaki pants. Amazingly he looked twenty pounds thinner.

After "eggs over my hammy" at Denny's, they were en route to find one Mr. Harmon Edison. Rudy got his name from the security guard at Silky O'Sullivan's, called the Communications Sergeant back in Willoughby Hills, got the info they needed to find him and logged everything on the wanted poster. In addition to all Rudy's scribbling, Jose Garcia now had a faded crease right across his face and another cutting through his chin as a result of the stress of residing in Rudy's back pocket.

Harmon Edison's residence wasn't far from downtown. Morgan suspected Rudy might have exaggerated his wealth because the residential areas they went through were a little distressed. His doubts were relieved when they turned onto Tennessee Street. He had seen the neighborhood when he and Rudy arrived in Memphis. As they drove down Riverside Drive upon their arrival he saw the mansions perched on the bluffs overlooking the Mississippi River. Some of them were no less than 8,000 square feet of living space. Edison's home was three stories high with enormous windows spanning a distance from the lower level to the gabled rooftop. There were bronze I-beams naked to the light, supporting the three levels where ivy flowed from clay cauldrons, cascading from the upper level to the second tier to meander across the beams and finally lie resting on the bottom floor. Water rushed down a 60-foot glass column and spilled into a water feature where exotic fish swam among lily pads, pond grass and live cattails. They could see an open staircase with lustrous red oak banisters and crystal spindles with internal lighting that made them glisten like diamonds. The house was accessible from the back lawn on Tennessee Street., where it was encircled by a forged iron fence. A gated football length driveway sported a telephone box mounted for visitor contact.

Rudy pushed on the button, waited for a split second then hit it again. No one answered, but a large muscular black man stepped out of the gatehouse. He was wide across the shoulders like a man who had spent a lifetime pounding railroad spikes with a sledgehammer. He was no less than six and a half feet tall, wearing a black suit and tie and could easily have been dressed for a formal dinner party. Morgan and Rudy watched him without comment. Finally Rudy-always-stating-the-obvious said," There's some real money around this place."

Morgan nodded.

The man opened the gate and sauntered up with one hand in his pocket, seemingly without a concern in the world. He poked his head inside the car window and scanned the interior.

"So whose car is it?" he asked, looking at Rudy over his sunglasses.

"Mine," Rudy said.

"Then you'd be Rudopp Campbell?"

"Rudolph Campbell," Rudy said, correcting his pronunciation. "How'd ya know that?"

"Come on man, you thank you can pawk yo big ass in dis driveway and I can't find out who you are before I come down here? "

"Then you've got connections with the Department

of Motor Vehicles?"

"Motor vehicles, er anybody else too. Whatcha here fo?"

Rudy fetched the wanted poster and held it out the window.

"Oh, that, well come on," he said as he sauntered away with one hand still in his pocket.

"That dude is bigger than Shaq!" Rudy said, astonished by his enormous frame.

"I don't know how anybody could burglarize this place," Morgan said, as Rudy put the car in gear and started to follow. The security guard strolled in the middle of the driveway at a snail's pace. He changed his hand from his left pocket to the right in a casual manner and then finally rested both hands inside his pockets. Rudy and Morgan may as well have been paperboys as far as he was concerned.

Rudy was steaming inside. His ego was being roughened by the guard's indifference. He flaunted his insolence in their faces like a man who was invulnerable to anxiety. That in itself was an enviable trait, but Rudy was insulted.

Rudy was good-natured, but he wasn't immune to grumbling. They were there as uninvited guests and should have had little expectations but Rudy was accustomed to being respected for nothing more than wearing a police uniform for twenty-six years. He was a conscientious cop, and he did a respectable job, and respect is automatically bestowed upon the uniform without regard to who wears it. Rudy missed that. Morgan recognized it in himself too and guarded against it. It was easy to blow up about simple things, like being carded at the barricade on Beale Street. He

41

expected to be waved through like Obi-wan Kenobi, and when he was stopped it irritated him. Somewhere inside the pit where 25 years of his existence resided was a depository of everything he had been. The absence of the spontaneous respect the uniform elicits rings a feeling of loss.

"It's okay, Rudy. This guy doesn't know we've been sticking our necks out for other people for a quarter of a century."

"You got that right," Rudy said, half smiling.

The Shaq-like security guard waited as they got out of the car. "Rudopp, you wanna let me have a gander at that pea shooter you got in yo ankle holster."

"You got x-ray vision, too," Rudy muttered.

"No, but I ain't seen no Yankee cop who didn't have a little heater under his pant cuff."

Rudy surrendered the .380, and the guard popped out the clip, handed the gun back to him and tossed the clip into the car seat. "It'll be there on yo way out." He grinned, "nice shirt."

Morgan smiled knowingly. Rudy glanced back over his shoulder as the back door clicked and a sixty something woman answered the door. "Anderson contacted Mr. Edison regarding your arrival. He's waiting in the foyer."

As they stepped inside, Morgan was astounded. The staircase they had seen through the windows from outside coiled its way around the brass I-beams, and the ivy found its way between the crystal spindles at several locations. There were live plants tenant upon every windowsill, and fresh flowers sprung from every nook and crevice. The floors and trim were sleek red oak, honed to perfection. Red granite tiles were arranged in the middle of the room, supporting a massive tufted maroon leather couch, and a substantial glass coffee table. Mr. Edison was comfortably settled, wearing black silk pajamas and sipping coffee from a clear glass mug. The foyer was bigger than Rudy's house.

Anyone with an ounce of perception could see that Morgan and Rudy were overwhelmed by the enormity and pretentiousness of it. Edison quietly appraised their behavior.

"It's a man's house," he said. "If there were a woman's influence here the ivy would be gone, the oak floors would be white marble and the trim would be delicate French whittle. And God knows my poor koi would have gone down the garbage disposal long ago."

"Nice," Rudy said, sounding as though he ambled around in places like this every day.

"What may I do for you gentlemen?"

Morgan waited for Rudy to start jabbering about the Mexican invasion, but he was speechless. Morgan waited but Rudy remained mum.

How did I get to be spokesman? Morgan thought to himself. Wasn't this all Rudy's idea? Finally Morgan started. "We weren't expecting an audience," he said, immediately hating himself for trying to sound pretentious. "But we were interested in the Jose Garcia burglary case. I'm a private detective from Illinois. I usually don't get involved in criminal cases, but we're both retired police officers and we read about the situation, and the possibility of a reward."

"Chicago, yes, a beautiful city," Edison said.

"Well, we're from Willoughby Hills."

Edison lowered his eyebrows in thought. I don't

43

believe I'm familiar with it," he said.

"It's on I-55 halfway between St. Louis and Chicago. We've got about thirty thousand people."

"Thirty-one," Rudy piped in.

Edison smiled.

At that point the conversation meandered aimlessly, with Edison commenting on how cold the winters were in Illinois, bemoaning how he was caught in a snowstorm near Joliet. His driver was blinded by a whiteout and they spent several hours stopped alongside the road waiting for the State Police to rescue them. They had to survive on champagne and soda crackers. "And by the way, isn't the city of Champaign and the University of Illinois located near you?" He asked, seemingly forgetting why they were there.

"Mr. Edison, what did Jose Garcia do?" Morgan asked, interrupting his monologue.

"He's taken something very valuable to me," Edison said. His demeanor immediately altered. He didn't have to grit his teeth or rant uncontrollably, the intensity borne in his gaze said it all. He was immediately darker and within himself.

"And I want it back!" he snapped.

Both Morgan and Rudy were silent. Edison's lips tightened into a rigid line, his brow furrowed, then in an instant his face brightened.

"Well, as it were. It's nice to talk to you gentlemen." He reached out to shake Rudy's hand, then to Morgan. "There's a twenty thousand dollar reward. Everybody knows about it. But if you're willing to work for me, I can make it more interesting. I'll have Anderson check out your credentials, and he'll call you tomorrow. You think about it. We'll see you then." He turned and crisply walked away.

As they were being escorted to the back door, Morgan glanced up and saw a beautiful girl sitting on the staircase. She looked to be about 18 or 19. Morgan's glance met her eyes. She was remarkably stunning. Her complexion was perfect, rich brown hair and her eyes were the deepest blue he'd ever seen. She made a cursory examination of him as she glided back up the staircase.

While the conversation between the two Illinois cops and Harmon Edison languished on, his security guard and his matronly house executive were in the study with their heads together with analytic caution discussing the new arrivals.

Anderson Claypool and Thelma Carlisle had a secret riding upon the sway. America had become a different place than the country where everything had been safe, where societal norms coincided with good intentions and national pride. Now everything was being assaulted by indifference and ambiguity. People believed America too big to fail; that the continual chipping away at her values and mores would never bring her down. Anderson and Thelma knew there were forces poised to bring her to her knees. In historical terms there were people who scoffed at the possibility of the disintegration of the Roman Empire even as the vandals were at the gate and sat in disbelief among the ruins after it had been reduced to rubble. The same thing might be awaiting the United States.

That's where Anderson's mind was fixed, but he didn't intend to leave her fate in the hands of politicians. Anderson had put wheels on his intentions and Morgan Cooper and Rudy Campbell were about to be drawn into the fray." Lives change", Anderson, muttered to himself as he watched them getting into Rudy's car. "Mine did and so will yours."

Once Morgan and Rudy were back in the car en route downtown, they talked about how unusual their meeting with Edison had been. He wasn't at all curious about them. He talked more about Illinois weather than he did about the fugitive Jose Garcia. He was open about not having a female influence in his house, yet when they were leaving a girl old enough to be an influence was quite evident on the staircase. Morgan was suspicious. Rudy wasn't concerned. "Aren't all rich people a little on the eccentric side?"

A couple of days passed and they became more acquainted with the humongous guard, Anderson. He never stopped being obnoxious with his pure undisguised ridicule and counterfeit patronization, he whittled away at their patience. They believed he clearly thought they were just the typical rural Andy and Barney type cops whose likelihood of actually producing results were slim to none. And if they did miraculously stumble onto something, they would mess it up, but yet strangely he was pushing them towards something. Rudy would have given him a little counseling if he had been anything less than raw muscle wrapped around bone. Morgan was more patient, or did he actually agree with Anderson: They actually were existentially out of place They didn't know that everything Anderson was doing was just an act.

When they left Willoughby Hills Morgan couldn't have been less interested in chasing down Jose Garcia. It was just the diversion. But now, here in Memphis,

his curiosity was being slightly kindled. Being nettled by Anderson didn't affect him. He didn't like being insulted or underrated, but that was a reality he accepted. People who lived in cities thought things were different in Mayberry, but the truth was that less people meant less cops. In the end it accounted for equal trouble. A serious situation in a small town was no different than a serious situation in a large city.

When the preliminaries were finished, Anderson gave Morgan $5,000 cash, and promised five more each week until they reached a dead end or produced Jose Garcia, and that would garner twenty thousand additional dollars. They were provided with a cell phone exclusively to report their findings every other evening at 9:00 p.m. sharp. No other communication would be necessary, and they were never to contact Mr. Edison directly.

This actually might be real detective work, according to Rudy, but Morgan was skeptical. "What's with no personal contact with Edison? Why cash? Why are we taking orders from a man who treats us like idiots when he's the one who says, "Talk at me ev'ah two days and don't be pester'n Mista Edison hisself."

Still in spite of his doubt, Morgan could feel his interest being fanned. At first it had been like an ember smoldering beneath the surface, and now it was a tiny little flame. Was it possible that he could think about something besides Molly? Maybe it was just the peculiarity of the situation that piqued his interest. Jose Garcia had broken into a fancy mansion with tight security, stolen something valuable, fled to Florida, and now Edison had more or less hired two strangers right off the street to go find him. He trusted them with $5,000 cash, but he didn't think it was necessary to tell them what Garcia had taken from him. His wealth was ostentatiously on display in his home, but his Chief of Security was illiterate, although probably more than capable for what was expected of him. He was certainly big enough.

They left Memphis on I-55 heading south, passing through Southaven, Mississippi. They had planned to get an early start but it was already 2:00 p.m. before they hit the road

"That's where John Grisham went to high school," Rudy noted. "Maybe he'll write a book about us chasin' old Joe Garcia."

"Right." Morgan said.

"There's a lot of famous people from Mississippi. John Grisham, Greg Isles, Morgan Freeman, and Oprah. A lot of others too."

"There's a lot of famous people from Illinois," Morgan added.

"Oh, yeah, name one." Rudy spouted.

"How about Lincoln, Grant, Reagan and Barack Obama?"

"Okay, I'll give ya that."

Chapter Five

I-55 runs through the Mississippi Delta; a place that is flat, fertile, and flush with cotton fields. It's a place where heat and humidity combine to create volatile weather conditions. A good place to find a storm.

Rudy's 2012 Lincoln town car was a good ride, and the talk radio program Rudy had chosen was blaring. They hit a two-lane highway south of Senatobia heading east across the state to Alabama. The sky was darkening in the southwest, and clouds were beginning to climb into the atmosphere. Thunder was rumbling in the distance, but it couldn't compete with the noise coming from the radio. Rudy grumbled and disagreed with the radio host, complained about the Mexican invasion, and condemned politicians in general. Morgan watched the scenery as the flatlands turned into rolling hills, and pastures. There were cattle ranches and horse stables along the roadways. An occasional southern mansion popped onto the landscape, but small one-story homes, and double wide trailers were more abundant. The hills were covered with brown grass and dust, and the fields were under attack from a savage onslaught of weeds. A cardboard sign was propped against a tree urging, "Lord, give us rain."

Flashes of lightning were becoming visible over the

tree line, and even with the radio booming inside the car, the thunder was rumbling loud enough to be heard. Trees were thick along the highway blocking the sky from view, but above the hills the atmosphere was turning a yellowish green color. Treetops rustled and sudden wind gusts streamed dust and debris across the roadway. The static on Rudy's AM radio program had become so intense that he had to turn it off.

"We might get a little rain," he said.

"Looks like it." Morgan agreed.

Just then they came upon an opening in the trees and on the horizon the sky was black with tremendous lightning bolts glowing and sprawling across the heavens. In an instant the light faded and a dark green veil enshrouded the land. It was four-thirty, but it was as dark as night.

"I don't like the looks of this," Morgan said.

"I didn't hear no storm warnings."

"You had the radio tuned to WLS out of Chicago. I was amazed you could get it this far south. But I know they wouldn't have weather coverage for this part of the country."

Rudy drove on, and the wind died down. An eerie quiet settled in for a moment, then large raindrops started falling. The windshield wipers were flapping quickly across the glass, but the rain was coming in waves.

"I need to pull over," Rudy said quietly, almost as though he were talking to himself.

"You got that right." Morgan said.

The rain came in torrents and pea-sized hail began to dance across the car hood. Both Rudy and Morgan searched the roadside for a place to stop. The car crawled along at a snail's pace as the hail got incrementally bigger, and soon it was thumping violently on the rooftop. The wind increased and large leaves and dust hovered overhead. Morgan saw a gravel road off to the right. He shouted, then banged Rudy's shoulder and pointed. Rudy swerved, hit the gravel and scooted across a bridge made of railroad ties. The wind howled and the debris and rain blew parallel to the ground. Morgan looked to the horizon, and to his horror they were directly in the pathway of an enormous black funnel, wrapped in hail, leaves and tree limbs. It was coming over the hillside, writhing and pitching from side to side. Shingles were sailing through the air like missiles and a deafening roar sounded more like the rumbling of a jet engine. The ground vibrated from the sound, and the wind pushed the car sideways.

"We gotta get out," Rudy bellowed.

Morgan didn't have to be told. He already had one foot on the ground and was headed for the ditch. As he slid into the ravine he saw a man and woman running towards him. Metal strips from the mobile home they had abandoned were swirling behind them like helicopter blades in the wind. Rudy hit the gravel road and bounced like a rubber ball into the ditch. The other two dove in behind him and they all scrambled under the wooden bridge. The noise was horrific. Rudy's car was lifted into the air and hovered momentarily, then it settled softly into the ravine. The mobile home exploded like it had been hit by a bomb and metal siding went up into the cloud rumbling and screeching. Two-by-fours bounced violently across the ditch and a piece of siding scooted up under the bridge miraculously passing between their necks and the bridge supports. They all hung onto each other as the wind tore at their clothing stinging their faces and bodies alike. Then the dust and debris pummeled them into the ground. The bridge rattled and heaved as pieces of loose boards fled in an upward spiral. The water in the ditch rose, soaking their ankles and shoes. The woman screamed, the man prayed. Morgan was later astounded that he had the presence of mind to note that his prayers were in Spanish. "God save us," the woman shouted in broken English.

The roaring lessened, and the rain came again in a deluge. Tree limbs could be heard breaking and snapping, but the overwhelming noise was gone. The rain slowed to a sprinkle as the four terrified humans slowly crept out from beneath the wooden bridge. They came out of their holes reminiscent of frightened little animals breathing a relieved sigh. They fell to their knees thanking God that they were saved.

Rudy rested his hands on his hips and surveyed the damage. Morgan tried to talk to the man and woman. They were Hispanic and didn't understand his words but they knew he was concerned.

"Are you alright?"

"Si," the man said, wiping his hand across his forehead, smiling, then whistled his relief.

The tin siding was wrapped around trees and hanging in the limbs above them. The mobile home was gone, leaving only a few concrete blocks, an old tire, and some steel fence post on the ground where they had been stuffed under the trailer for safe keeping. Clothes and furniture littered the ground for three hundred yards, mixed with roofing, insulation and building materials from other places swept in by the tornado.

"I've never been that scared before," Rudy said, shaking his head at the desolation. He was still trembling.

"It sure was some scary crap," Morgan agreed. He thought about how he prayed every night to disappear into the abyss. It was glaringly obvious that he had his opportunity, but he ran for his life, and hovered in fear of losing it. Obviously, he wanted to live.

Within twenty minutes the rain was completely gone. Muddy water rushed through the ditch carrying unidentifiable items and trash downstream. The earlier noted cardboard sign saying," Lord give us rain," washed under the bridge headed south.

Morgan and Rudy tried in vain to push the car out of the ditch while the Mexicans rummaged through the debris trying to salvage clothing and other necessities. They each carried a plastic Walmart bag crammed with things they had taken away from the scene. Their expressions said it all. Everything they had in the world was stuffed in the Walmart sacks.

A man in a yellow rain suit came across the hill. He explained that he was sent by the county to help clear the downed trees and search for injured people. He said there had been three funnels and the devastation was far-reaching. The highway was blocked in both directions for several miles. He could get the car out of the ditch with his bobcat, but they would be stuck there until morning. He assured them that he would return but it would be awhile before he could get to his equipment to make the return trip.

The rain stopped and darkness descended. Morgan and Rudy tried to sit in the car, but their added weight caused the car to inch farther into the ravine. They found an uprooted tree where they sat, wet and cold. The Mexicans joined them. The four of them were lined up on the log silently watching the sky as the clouds cleared and the white light of the moon cast eerie shadows across the saturated meadow.

In little more than an hour Rudy was beginning to recover. He paced in front of the log eyeballing the Mexicans in quick glances. "Have you got your papers?" he asked.

"No habla Englise, Senore."

"Your Passport, you savie?"

"No comprendo, Amigo."

"Papers, papers, you know," he said, demonstrating a writing motion in the air."

Both the man and woman studied him in total bewilderment for a short time, then the man seemed to get it. "Oh, si, pepoors, si."

Morgan wore a subdued smile. Rudy didn't have the authority to arrest a duck, much less enforce federal immigration laws. But he was being Rudy. There was the right way, the wrong way, and Rudy's way.

The little Mexican fellow hurried to the rubbish pile which was once their home and started digging. His wife joined him. Soon they were back with a few pieces of dry paper. The woman had located a gas lighter. Together they scurried around picking up sticks and leaves. Morgan realized they were gathering materials for a fire, so he joined them. They found some field rocks and made a circle for a fire pit. The little man placed the paper beneath the limbs and after a couple of false starts they had a fire blazing.

Morgan chuckled, "Good idea, Rudy. It never hurts

to have a little dry paper lying around when you need a fire."

As the sky grew darker and the moon and stars brighter, every manner of animal noises emanated from the woods. Rudy was up talking to the Mexicans as if they could understand. He told them about his life on the police department, showed them his badge. He and Morgan were lifelong friends, "didn't ya know," and they had played baseball and basketball on the same teams. Morgan struck out in the 9th inning with the tying run on third base, and he drove him in with a sac fly. That was in the regionals back in 1965.

The couple watched him as if they understood every word. Occasionally one of them would smile and nod. The woman returned to the rubble and retrieved a half empty bottle of strawberry wine. They passed it around. Rudy went for it without hesitation and Morgan followed but not quite without thinking he might be immediately putrefied. He swallowed hard the first round, but subsequent passes were smoother.

Rudy collected blankets from the car trunk to spread on the ground around the fireside where it had dried. As the fire burned lower they slept, huddled together like a family of dogs.

As promised, the man in the yellow rain suit returned at morning light with his bobcat. In short order the car was back on the roadway. It was mechanically sound, but the paint resembled the skin of a golf ball. After standing around taking in the devastation in the harsh daylight, they were even more overwhelmed. Rudy was on the cell phone with his insurance man and the Mexican couple were standing in the gravel lane that had been their driveway less than

24 hours earlier. The man's salt and pepper hair, in total disarray, protruded from beneath his John Deere cap, his whiskers already in need of a shave, and the mud caked his long-sleeved white shirt and khaki pants. The woman was equally disheveled. The mud pancakes on her dress were as prominent as the enormous flower print. She was wearing a shoe on one foot and a brown wool sock on the other. The bulging Walmart bags were dangling at their sides.

"We'll see ya, Pedro," Rudy said.

Morgan gave Rudy a perturbed glance. "Knock it off, Rudopp."

"That's his name, Morgan!"

"His name is Pedro?"

"Yes, and hers is Maria."

"You're kidding me."

"Nope, they told me last night. You was out getting wood, and he said, "Me Pedro, she Maria.""

Pedro watched them trying to get the drift, but it was plain to see he didn't understand a word. He smiled, but his eyes were quietly pleading. Maria's face was drawn, worry prominent.

"We can't leave them here, Rudy." Morgan said.

"I knew it!" Rudy shouted. "I knew you'd be bleeding all over the place for them. I knew it!"

"They don't have any place to go."

"They don't have papers. We'd be aiding illegal immigrants."

Morgan was quiet. Rudy got out of the car and opened the back door. "Get in Pedro-Maria. Hop right in there. Have a good time on old Rudy."

Back in Memphis, Harmon Edison and Anderson Claypool were walking down Turnbold Street en route to the Edison House for Homeless Girls, a place where young woman and girls could take refuge from the streets. For the latter part of the twentieth century it had been a hospital, but Edison purchased it when the new hospital was erected, renovated it and transformed it into a home for young women. There were street prostitutes, delinquents, and abandoned children living there. The home bore his name, but he was totally low-key about it. He shunned the limelight. He never gave interviews or sought recognition for his generosity. Girls were rehabilitated from drug use, rescued from broken homes, and fetched from the underworld of the streets. Occasionally he showed up there unannounced, took a look around, and made small talk with the staff, never offered opinion or interfered with the operation.

Today the sun was shining and the air was clear. The trees on Turnbold Street hinted an early autumn. It was warm but the previous evenings storms had wrung out the humidity and the air was fresh and crisp. Edison was dressed in a finely tailored suit and imported Italian shoes. Anderson was dressed in his usual black suit and tie. He was a head taller than Edison.

Just as they approached the entrance to Edison House, they met a middle-aged man who was digging into a folder rummaging through what appeared to be a pile of unorganized paperwork. His head was down and he walked directly into Edison with a jolt. He was surprised and momentarily both he and Edison were knocked off balance. When they looked at each other, a peculiar expression was abruptly evident on Edison's face. The other man's initial shock gave way to recognition. He was momentarily without words. His mouth was gaped open, and his eyes firmly fixed on Edison's face.

"Charley Heidbreider!"

"I'm sorry," Edison said politely.

"Charley, what the hell! I haven't seen you in twenty-five years.

"I'm sorry, but you must be mistaken," Edison replied.

The man was dressed in rumpled Dockers, shoes that might have been castoffs from a bowling alley, a brown plaid jacket, and a soiled thin brown tie. His belt was several loops too long by the way the end flopped about. Not only his fashion sense but his social graces were sorely lacking evidenced by his face-talking and unkept fingernails extended to Edison. At any rate, he wouldn't have traveled in the same circles with Edison.

"Wow, Charley, the used car business must be booming," he said as he examined Edison's clothing.

"I don't know you, so please excuse me," Edison said as he tried to push past him. The man still persisted, but Anderson stepped between them.

"Now Mista Edison done said he don't know you, so you need to move on down da street."

Edison stepped into the doorway at Edison House, and he and Anderson disappeared inside. Bewildered the man muttered, "What the hell!" as he slowly meandered away.

Chapter Six

Pedro and Maria were like two scruffy puppies. They were impossible to cast off. They didn't want to leave the car, and when it was suggested, they pretended not to get it. They poked around in their Walmart bags, looked out the window, or busied themselves in various ways avoiding eye contact with Rudy or Morgan. Rudy was trying to be the bad guy, cursing and complaining, knowing it was falling on deaf ears. Morgan could see in Rudy's eyes that he wasn't going to throw them to the wolves. They had intended to take them to the next town and drop them, but as things turned out, they drove through Mississippi, hit Alabama, then went south through Mobile where they caught I-10 east. It was midnight when they reached Jacksonville, Florida. Pedro and Maria were still with them. The back seat and floor were cluttered with McDonald's hamburger wrappers, and the two of them were snoring quietly. Morgan checked into the Tradition Inn, purchasing three rooms with the first portion of the $5,000 Anderson had given him. He and Anderson hadn't discussed any record keeping, but he saved the receipts to account for his spending.

Rudy unloaded the baggage. When he was finished and ready to go inside he pointed south and said,

"Mexico is that a-way." Pedro and Maria stared at him blankly. Their limp little bodies stood motionless. Rudy pondered silently, then said, "Come on. I know old bleed'n heart has a room for ya." Their expressions changed immediately. Rudy's words were English, but his body language was Hispaniola.

The palm trees alongside the parking lot were stirring with the breeze and a pale moon peeked through a thin layer of clouds. Rudy was settled in and Pedro and Maria were sitting on their balcony. Pedro was smoking a cigar while Maria jabbered incessantly. In ten minutes Maria had spoken more words than she had said in 700 miles. She didn't know Morgan was strolling around the parking lot within hearing distance. She was set free from the thrall of being at the mercy of strangers, her anxiety fled the instant she and Pedro were alone. Now the comfort of her own words and Pedro's undivided attention came over her in waves. She stopped talking only to laugh, then she would begin again.

Although Morgan was there with Rudy, there was still an alien sense of being meandering around inside his head. Just a few years ago his entire life was laid out in a neat little package. It was so mundane and routine. He would kiss Molly on his way out the door on his way to have coffee with his old retired friends, then saddle up the old Hyundai and head out to serve a few papers. He might have a beer at Old Joe's with Rudy, then go home and mow the grass. Molly would dig in the flower garden while he watched. Later they would have a glass of wine near the fountain before they retired inside to watch TV. That was all there was and he was satisfied with it. He didn't think about growing old, or long for his lost youth. He just wanted another day just like the last one.

Now he didn't know what to think. He deliberated for a moment as he stood there under the full moon watching the palm trees swaying in the wind. In less than a week he had hung out the moon in a world famous bar, defended himself from a robbery attack and relieved his would-be robbers of their last pennies, not to mention splitting one of their heads open with a zap. He had taken a job from a stranger he knew nothing about, cowered in a ditch while a tornado ravaged everything in sight, and now he was holed up in a hotel with Rudy and two illegal Mexican immigrants. Life certainly doesn't telegraph its punches. Everything changes, whether you want it to or not.

In addition to all that, he was contracted to find a man who might be anywhere in North America. He wasn't prepared mentally, he didn't have connections, and his training was, as they say, geared to finding doughnuts. In spite of all that, there was something stirring in that secluded place inside where it's neither the mind nor the body. He could feel it bouncing around touching every particle of his being. He felt like he had just found something more, and it was exhilarating. It was a "high," that he didn't understand. Maybe there is something inside a human being that regenerates the will to live; to move beyond a life-crushing tragedy and begin again. Maybe it was that perplexing ingredient propelling him into the unknown. Maybe he and Rudy could actually accomplish something from this. He wasn't naive, nor was he given to fits of fancy, so his head wasn't full of thoughts of glory. He knew he and

Rudy were just small town cops without real credentials, and Jose Garcia wasn't an anti-superhero. He was wholly aware he was treading on new territory. As he slipped beneath the covers, he was excited by the prospect of tomorrow.

As the morning sun glistened on the ocean, Morgan, Rudy, Pedro and Maria cruised south on I-95 in Rudy's hail-ravaged Lincoln Town car. Getting rid of their Mexican guests wasn't a concern for Morgan or Rudy at the moment. They were like a faint headache, slightly nagging but so insignificant that they were endured in lieu of being treated. Finding a place to unload them was like getting up in the middle of the night to find an aspirin. At that point they were just easier to ignore.

Rudy's stomach was rumbling and he wanted to get off the interstate to find a restaurant with eggs dotted with pepper riding on the grease from the grill, milk gravy, biscuits with sausage, and a pile of fried potatoes covered with salsa. They didn't have a breakfast on the interstates that would put you in your coffin like a good greasy spoon from back home. You had to hit the two lanes to find something like that.

Pedro and Maria were beginning to know when it was time to eat by the way Rudy eyeballed every restaurant advertisement along the roadway. They perked up, astute to the fact they would be fed soon.

Open air fruit stands with cascading shelves of oranges and Vidalia Onions crowded against the road. Cars from Ohio, Michigan, and Illinois filled the gravel parking lots and women walked in vacant lots with little yapping dogs, sniffing and squatting without regard to passing cars.

Rudy guided the car into a parking spot in front of a rundown fruit stand where the wheels of commerce had apparently ground to a stop. There was one lone patron who was sniffing cantaloupes, and squeezing peaches, but aside from her the less than appealing fruit place was empty. Morgan didn't question Rudy, but he knew fruit wasn't a dietary necessity for Rudy. In addition to the eatables, there were two rounders loaded with discount clothing and a pile of used shoes. Rudy didn't sniff the cantaloupe. He headed straight for the clothing. He motioned for Pedro and Maria to join him. Together they fanned through the clothing, and after a short time Rudy sent Pedro and Maria to the try-on shed behind the fruit stand. When they returned Pedro was wearing a long sleeved Jonas brothers t-shirt, used Old Glory jeans, and a pair of Nitro jogging shoes. Maria had a Run DMC sweatshirt and jeans shorts with an emblazoned purple embroidery star on the hip pocket. Rudy dropped the old clothes into the garbage barrel on his way back to the car.

Now that Pedro and Maria were better dressed, or at least clean, they found a nice Starv'n Marvin type greasy spoon. Morgan glanced at Rudy sideways a few times before he finally spoke. "What goes through your mind, Rudy? Last week you wanted to skin alive every Mexican you saw, and now you're Big Daddy. I know I'm just as involved with them as you, but hell, wasn't I supposed to be the bleeding heart?"

"I just don't want 'em gett'n my car any dirtier than they already have. The back seat smells like the monkey house at the zoo."

"Okay, sure, whatever." Morgan said.

The restaurant they found was an old converted gas

station with booths and tables covered in red and white checkered tablecloths, and a counter with little short round stools. It wasn't any different than many dumps like it in Illinois. Wasn't Florida supposed to be Floridian-like? Amazingly, the place was full. The waitress told them to be seated as she hurried past them with two plates and a tray full of hot coffee. They took the only remaining booth, and soon she was back for their order.

Pedro took off his John Deere hat and his thick salt and pepper hair dropped below his ears.

"Boy, you Mexicans sure have some thick hair," Rudy said. Being lucky enough to have a full healthy head of hair himself, Rudy frequently compared his own mop to other men his age. He liked the superiority of being fully endowed. Pedro was dumb to the statement, but he smiled.

They were seated in the back near the restroom doors but it wasn't the worst seat in the house. That seat was occupied by a scruffy guy who looked like he might have paved the "road to perdition" all by himself. He had long dirty blond hair, a dark blue t-shirt with a hole just below the pocket, worn out jeans, and cowboy boots. He looked to be about 35 and badly in need of a shave. He was smoking right under the "no smoking" sign, and occasionally he sipped from a whiskey bottle he concealed in his rear pocket. He was a man who raged against the world. He was someone who had seen some hard times, but probably most by his own making. A snarl held reign over his features implying that it was someone else's fault. Bitter and mean, it didn't matter whose fault it was, when he was provoked he was as dangerous as a rattlesnake.

He would be hard not to notice if you were within sight. The waitress clearly appeared cautious bordering on nervous. It was obvious they knew one another, maybe they even had a relationship. When she meekly asked him to stop smoking, he reached for her arm. She backed away and said they would talk later. She glanced around mindful of who might be watching. He grumbled and crushed his cigarette on the floor.

It was an easy read for Morgan. There was trouble ahead. Just as a yawn travels around a room, so does trouble. It moves through crowds and settles upon unsuspecting people and marks them for unwanted participation. Sometimes it's mere inconvenience, but sometimes people get hurt. Sometimes people die. Most of the time trouble starts with a guy just like the man who was smoking beneath the "no smoking" sign.

Morgan watched him as his eyes followed the waitress around the room. It wasn't admiration or desire, but more anger and frustration. He wanted something from her that she wasn't giving up, maybe a smile and reassurance. Instead she was giving him reluctance and tentative glances. He wanted her to say, "Don't worry about me, baby, we're all good.," but her eyes were saying, "I can't do this anymore."

A deep sigh escaped the man's lips, his stare dropped to the floor, his eyes narrowed, and an expression of pure exasperation clutched him. He stomped his boot, pushed back his chair and started for the door.

Poor little Pedro; unsuspecting little Pedro had the misfortune of leaving his foot with his newly acquired Nitro jogging shoe in the pathway of a man looking for a target.

As the man marched by, his boot caught the tip of Pedro's shoe. He turned and his glare focused on Pedro. "Hey, Jose, get your foot out of the aisle!" he shouted.

Morgan saw his eyes. They were eyes filled with hatred and self-pity. They were eyes that couldn't see danger or assess reality. They were eyes that could only see a place for his fists to land, or for his boot to grind. He had found his target.

"Losiento," Pedro said.

"Speak English!" He snarled.

Morgan was trying to find his way past Rudy, but Rudy was already in action. As the man's fist headed for Pedro's face, Rudy's arm interceded. The blow knocked Rudy off balance and hot coffee, knives, forks, and chairs rattled across the floor. It was an unfair match up. Rudy's sixty-two-year-old overweight body compared to a wild man with adrenaline pumping through his veins spelled disaster. A second blow fell hard across Rudy's head. Morgan grabbed the man and they went down together. Morgan's back crackled and popped like a bowl of Rice Krispies, and pain shot up both arms. The man was back on his feet. He put a boot in Morgan's ribs. Rudy was struggling to get back into the fight when his nose hooked up with the business end of the man's knuckles.

The waitress darted across the restaurant and clutched at the man's back, shouting, "Jimmy, please, please stop!" A swift swipe of Jimmy's hand and she was sent sprawling across the floor.

****

Meanwhile back in Willoughby Hills, it was a quiet morning. The hot August days were gone and the September mornings were cool and bright. The leaves were just beginning to turn. Shades of orange and red were adorning the tips of the oak and maple leaves. Cars moseyed down the roads, and children laughed and giggled as they headed off to school. Willoughby Hills policemen drank coffee in Freda's Restaurant, and local citizens bid them good morning. Everything was good in Willoughby Hills, but in Mudville, Florida, things had gone asunder. Morgan and Rudy were hooked onto the losing end of an ass-kicking wagon.

Just when all seemed lost, Maria burst into action. She quickly grabbed a chair and slid it behind Jimmy's feet. Pedro popped up swinging. His hands were quick and his punches were true. His little fists pounded Jimmy's head and Jimmy stumbled backwards and tripped over the chair. Rudy, Morgan and Pedro were quick to pounce. They held Jimmy down as he kicked and growled like an angry dog. Things might have shaped up with Jimmy on his back and the other three holding him down, but it wasn't to be. Maria grabbed a fork from the table and stuck it between Jimmy's ribs. The shock registered on his face as a blood geyser quickly soaked his shirt.

Rudy's love for America conflicted with his dislike for change. He wanted his country to be like it was back in Willoughby Hills when he was growing up. He liked it when people obeyed the rules, worked hard, respected each other's property, and lived charitable lives. He didn't smoke, but he didn't want the government to dictate no smoking rules to private property owners. Greed rubbed him the wrong way but he thought progressive taxation was un-American. Welfare abuse was unacceptable and able-bodied men who demanded aid from the government were on Rudy's most worthless list. Illegal immigration was as cut and dry as day and night and there were no reasons for it, just excuses. In Rudy's world, everything was black and white. That is until that moment.

There on the front lines where the battle raged, the waters had muddied. He and Morgan were punching, kicking and bleeding for their little Mexican friends. He didn't believe in fleeing from the law, or thwarting the Constitution, but in that instant Rudy's bolt position had just crumbled. When the cops arrived it would make little difference how the fight had started, or who had started it. Pedro and Maria would be carted off to jail. Maria would probably be charged with a felony, and Pedro would be deported to Mexico. Maria would be alone to fend for herself.

Rudy pushed himself to his knees. He could feel the blood soaking through his shirt, slick and warm beneath his hands. Morgan was groaning and holding his ribs. Along with the blood splotches, the cruel realization of the situation was plastered on Pedro's face. Rudy's tightly bound package of rules had just been splintered. He looked at Pedro and said, "Run! Run Pedro! Vamose!

Pedro turned his palms out, as if to ask where.

Rudy was hysterical. "Vamose, Pedro! Get!"

One tug on Pedro's shirt by Maria was enough to jar loose the static idea that they were trapped, and in a moment they were out the door. Stunned patrons watched in amazement. Morgan grabbed a towel from the countertop and began applying pressure to the wound. Jimmy moaned and tried to get up. The waitress said, "Be still, Jimmy, you've been stuck."

Jimmy looked at her through grateful eyes as she stroked his hair, and he said, "Not again." In Jimmy's world where loneliness was inevitable, it wasn't going to get any better than that.

Tom Brewster

Chapter Seven

Morgan and Rudy were questioned by the police and released after a dozen patrons from the restaurant signed statements indicating that Jimmy was the instigator. A well-known troublemaker, most people thought his getting a fork in his ribs was a good thing, even overdue. Still the police would be seeking Pedro and Maria.

As Rudy drove past the Maid Rite Laundromat for the third time he grumbled. "Don't Mexicans always go to the laundromat when they don't have anywhere else to go!"

Morgan held his ribs and poked fun at Rudy's new facial makeup. He was wearing two black eyes and a band-aid across his nose. Morgan was certain that he had at least one broken rib and his tendonitis was working overtime. As things stood, he couldn't believe investigations required so much punching and kicking. They had roughed up two misfits in Memphis, and now they had their asses handed to them in grand fashion. They were batting .500. Chances were that if this "real detective work" continued on its path to-date, he'd be in a nursing home before his first $5,000 ran out.

Right at the moment he and Rudy had squandered the opportunity to lose their Mexican cohorts. Couldn't they just get into the car and drive away? Rudy had forgotten his repugnance for the Mexican invasion, and now he scanned every alley, every parking lot, desperate to find his Hispanic entourage. It was pitiful to watch.

The sun was blazing hot and it was nearly noon. They covered the town in its entirety three times. Had it been twenty, it wouldn't have mattered. Rudy wasn't giving up. The only communication between Rudy, Pedro, and Maria besides body language was the word, vamoose. Somehow that was the adhesive that came to bind them. Telling Pedro to run when it was against everything he believed in had pushed him into a new moral dimension. "Illegal immigrant" wasn't just symbolic terminology now There were real problems without cut and dried solutions.

Just like when you've lost your glove and you finally realize it's in your teeth, they saw four little feet protruding from under a bush they had passed four or five times already. Rudy glanced over his shoulder, looked in his rear view, and then slammed on the brakes. He popped out of the car and hurried to retrieve his friends. Morgan was standing beside the car smiling. Mother hen has found her chicks!

Rudy was tapping Pedro on the foot trying to hurry him before the police might round the corner. Pedro was busy gathering the oranges he and Maria had cultivated from a yard during their flight from justice. When you were on the lamb, it was important to eat right.

"Hey, leave the oranges. We ain't eatin' stolen fruit," Rudy snorted.

Just then a very believable replica of Jesus Christ himself came around the corner. A tanned face with

71

piercing blue eyes scrutinized the milieu from behind a beard and mustache complete with long brown hair. He was swaddled in a long robe and wore sandals straight from Babylon. The intensity of his stare might have scorched the earth, but they were spared when Maria shouted in Spanish, "He walks among us."

The man marched towards them shouting, "The end is near, repent and be saved." Maria fell to her knees and Pedro clasped his hands in prayer. Morgan was standing on the sidewalk, amused by the spectacle.

"This is the eleventh hour, cleanse your soul and be with the Lord in the end!"

Rudy was still nervous about the police. He had seen the end of the world several times in his sixty-two years and he wasn't concerned. He was worried, however, that a Jesus look-alike would attract the law. If that happened, Maria would be waiting bail, and Pedro would be on his way to Mexico.

As the prophet passed by Morgan he leaned his head in and said, "Jose Garcia frequents the Nets End Tavern in the Hispanic district west of Hollywood - evenings at about six thirty." It didn't register immediately what had happened. A smile crossed Morgan's face as he watched the man cross the street and disappear around the corner of a building. Then it hit him.

"What?"

Rudy glanced at Morgan as he stuffed Pedro and Maria into the car. "I didn't say anything."

"No, Jesus said it."

"Jesus said, what, but it came out of your mouth."

"No, he said, Jose Garcia frequents the Nets End Tavern."

"How does Jesus know that?" Rudy spouted in

disbelief.

How did he even know they were looking for Jose Garcia? Rudy was stoned-faced as he analyzed what had happened.

"Get in! We gotta find Jesus," Morgan shouted.

They were off in a cloud of dust, to search every alley and vacant lot in the town, but the search was futile. The prophet had either ascended to a higher plane or had ditched his robe and sandals and scrammed. Either way, they had missed him.

They talked about how strangely things were coming down. Morgan reckoned that he had crossed over into a parallel universe or had occupied someone else's life. Two weeks ago he was thinking he might take a few days off to go fishing, and maybe he would volunteer at the American Legion's monthly bingo. He wouldn't call the numbers but he thought he could help with the prizes or check the cards for accuracy. "We've got a bingo here, Bob. It's a winner!"

As they drove back to the interstate Pedro and Maria sat quietly in the back seat. They were happy to still be in the fray, but they were totally clueless, as were Morgan and Rudy. Where had Jesus come from, and how did he know their situation? He had to have been sent by someone who had an interest in what they were doing. They agreed that they wouldn't tell Anderson because it was too strange to think he had sent a Son of God impersonator to tell them that Jose Garcia frequents the Nets End Tavern. At that moment it was information better kept amongst themselves.

They didn't stop to analyze the new wrinkle. They made their way back to I-95 and went south. They drove in silence and watched the scenery. It had been many years since Morgan had been to Florida. The waves steadily lapping against the beach, the sea oats, and the sails on the wind in the distance propelled him to that brief time when he lived his life in the moment. He and Molly stayed for a month at Grand Shores West at Reddington Beach. Molly's "Uncle Bob" was the maintenance man there and generously allowed them to stay in a condo free of charge. The owner of the place was in Europe and didn't know he was sporting a couple of freeloaders. Morgan was twenty-four and Molly was twenty-one. A vision of Molly was imprinted clearly in his memory. The silvery moon was positioned in the evening sky shining over the ocean as the waves thundered on the beach. She was wearing a half sleeve white shirt and the breeze was blowing her long brown hair across her face, as the lunar glow glistened in her eyes. She was so young and beautiful that the thought of that evening caused Morgan's stomach to tingle and his heart was unleashed. He studied Rudy's face knowing there wasn't a mean particle in his body. Morgan was glad his big dumb friend was there. If not, at that moment he would have come unhinged.

Rudy was whistling a tune by the Eagles. His cheeks were full of air and as the high pitches in the song were completed, he opened up and sang "Ain't it hard to be all alone in the center ring when there's no time left to borrow." He laughed and reached across the seat and smacked Morgan's shoulder. "It's good to be alive, huh, Morgan." Pedro and Maria were smiling, not understanding a word, but knowing that brotherhood was alive and well in Mudville.

Chapter Eight

In Collinsville, Illinois, a world away from where Morgan and Rudy were, Bashaar Amir, a Syrian immigrant, was planning treachery. He arrived in the United States on December 13, 2003, the same day Saddam Hussein was routed from his hole by US forces near Tikrit, Iraq. Bashaar's cousin was a successful businessman in Collinsville, where he owned several gas stations, apartment buildings and a facility housing a vocational college. Most of his success was supplemented by the United States Government. His cousin got into the country with help from another cousin, and there were others who arrived in the same manner. Critics call it chain migration. Bashaar received a minority government loan and start-up money from Uncle Sam through the Small Business Administration. By the time Saddam Hussein's neck was stretched by the Saudis on December 30th, 2006, Bashaar owned three low rent hotels on I-55 just across the Mississippi River from St. Louis. In 2009 he brought his father, Ekton, and brother, Ahmed, in from Syria. They were all radicalized Muslims and believed in a worldwide caliphate. As time passed they were involved in providing transportation and lodging for recruits who were en route to Iraq and Syria to join ISIS. In 2013 their mission had evolved into plotting stateside bombings. Although Bashaar was yet to actively participate he had rolled over the thought of taking out the St. Louis Arch. However, after researching the logistics of actually bringing it down, he learned that it was so structurally sound that it was impossible to build a bomb powerful enough to do the job. He also considered an attack on Busch Stadium or the St. Louis Zoo, but settled on a plan to truck bomb Laclede's Landing after a Cubs/Cardinal game. He and his brother, Ahmed, formed a team of radicals which included an M.D who practiced out of St. Elizabeth's Medical Group in Belleville, Illinois, two locals who worked as hotel clerks, and an Airman from Scott Air Force Base.

Laclede's Landing was a historic area on the Mississippi River, a touristy hangout with narrow granite paved roads with bottleneck access for hundreds of out-of-towners to gather before and after the St. Louis Cardinal games. Security on the Landing was nonexistent, making it a perfect location to do some real damage and kill hundreds, maybe even a thousand people. It's the oldest part of St. Louis, dating back to the time when William Clark was governor of the Missouri Territory and has been restored to its original architecture. A place in time where restaurants and bars have an old world flavor, and most are jammed on weekends and games days. Destroying historic buildings and killing a thousand unsuspecting people would be monumental, right there in the nation's heartland.

Radical Islamic immigrants were in businesses throughout Illinois in hotels, grocery stores and gas stations. Some of them were suspected of having contacts with terrorist organizations and were under surveillance by Homeland Security but there were hundreds who were not and could be called upon without drawing suspicion.

Bashaar's contacts included a man who worked for a farm supply store in Springfield, Illinois. He was familiar with the rural farms and fertilizer suppliers throughout the state. He put Bashaar onto a location where thousands of 50 pound bags of ammonium nitrate were stored. The only security was a single video camera streaming back to the office computer in a little town of Lowder, Illinois. It had one street, a fertilizer plant, and a feed mill. The computer was left in the office when the secretary went home and even when the office was occupied it wasn't monitored.

The storage shed containing the fertilizer was six miles from the fertilizer plant on a one-lane dirt road in the middle of a soybean field. In central Illinois the land is so flat that you can see small towns that dot the landscape from ten miles away. This place was so remote that in the dark of night it was hard to see a light. It was a perfect place to acquire enough fertilizer to blow Laclede's Landing into the Mississippi River.

Bashaar acquired a box truck from a junkyard in East St. Louis, Illinois. It was impounded by the Illinois State Police for having been used to transport a cache of marijuana from south Texas en route to Chicago. It was apprehended just north of Edwardsville, Il, and eventually sold on auction. It was in good shape but could not be licensed for the road. It had a junk title, but that was little concern to Bashaar. He had it professionally painted with The Old Spaghetti House logo, a popular restaurant on the landing, attached stolen plates and made a couple of successful dry runs down Morgan Street in Laclede's to see if it attracted attention.

Now Bashaar's plan was to send his brother and two other co-conspirators to steal enough ammonium nitrate to obliterate the Landing. They would simply drive the box truck to Lowder, Illinois, break into the fertilizer shed and take the ammonium nitrate back to Collinsville and park it behind the Impire Inn, Bashaars hotel, and his residence, and wait for the appropriate moment to execute the plan. Simple detonating devices much like those used by Timothy McVeigh in the Oklahoma City bombing of the Edward Morrow building were ready to install. Ahmed would drive the van down the cobblestone street and park it in front of the Morgan Street Bar. He would leave the truck and Bashaar would pick him up. They would proceed to a location on Washington Street before detonating the bomb. A hundred bags of fertilizer would take out everything on both sides of the street for an entire block. There would be enough blood and destruction to send a chill down the spine of America. People would know there was no safe place anywhere in the country. It was a good plan. Praise Allah!

Chapter Nine

Anderson Claypool was standing at the gate of the Harmon Edison estate dressed in black fatigues. The city lights were glowing in the low hanging clouds. The gray light of dawn on the Memphis skyline was breaking to usher in a dreary, misty morning. What Anderson was about to do was no more than an errand for him, but it would take at least twenty four hours. Soldiers who patrolled the streets of Kabul and police officers working in the most dangerous inner cities in America might be anxious in Anderson's position, but he was as quiet and calm as a Sunday morning prayer meeting.

A black suv stopped at the gate . Anderson hopped in and the driver stepped out and walked away, leaving Anderson with the car. After several minutes he was southbound on I-55 passing through Southhaven Mississippi. The clouds blocked the sun as the gray morning light revealed long flat cotton fields stretching endlessly into the Mississippi delta. Occasionally a tree line full of hedge apples popped up to separate one field from another but aside from that the landscape was an uneventful expanse of monotony.

A few miles out of Hernando, Mississippi, Anderson left the interstate for a dusty road where a single engine Cessna 206 was parked at the end of a long grassy runway. Anderson had only three full days training in the cockpit of an airplane but he was intelligent and capable. Learning how to fly was as easy for him as riding a bike. Within minutes he was airbound headed for a small makeshift runway located on a farm in Mason County, Illinois. When he landed three hours later dense clouds had gathered and the ground was blanketed with air so heavy a white haze had formed in layers above the fields. It had rained earlier and it would rain again before the day was through, but it didn't matter to Anderson - good weather, bad weather, it was all the same to him.

A white Dodge 1500 hundred was waiting. A bearded man wearing a camouflage baseball cap and military fatigues, was in the driver's seat. When Anderson slid into the passenger seat the man extended his hand to shake. "I'm Bradley-----.

"Don't say it," Anderson interrupted. "I don't want to know your name. I' don't want to know your story - nothing. I don't want to know anything about you."

The man scowled and pulled the cap tighter on his head. "Whatever you say, boss," he said gruffly.

They drove in silence to Illinois Rt 10, headed east to connect with Route 29 south. The man in the baseball cap was wearing a beard, he was slightly overweight, about forty years old. His name was Bradley Lineweber. His hands were the size of hams, and there was a book on hard work and devotion contained within the lines and scars on those hardened knuckles. A silver chain with a cross hung on his thick neck. It was the only delicate thing about him. He was big, not as enormous as Anderson, but thick and brawny. His eyes were deep gray and held the characteristic of having lived through critical times.

Finally the big man spoke. "Buddy, we're all in this together," he said.

Anderson looked straight ahead. "That's true, we are. But my reasons and yours are different. I'm sure yours are valid, but I don't want the weight of other people's feelings interfering with what I need to do. I don't want to think about it."

"Fair enough," the big man said

Anderson turned to look at Lineweber. He had a round amiable face. The lines in his face were etched by worry and pain, but just as many defined by laughter too. Anderson suppressed the urge to talk. The less he knew the better. Before September 11, 2001, he was a different man. Talking and socializing was second nature to him then, but that part of him had been sapped in an instant. Now his actions were fed by anger, and he didn't want to diminish the intensity of his rage with conversation.

"You know I've been at this a long time," Anderson said quietly, momentarily giving in to his inclination for conversation.

Lineweber watched Anderson, his eyes full of questions.

"You know, someday they'll get to me. It's just a matter of time. They'll get you too if you stay with this," Anderson said.

"I'm doing this for God, my family, and my country, and there's no greater calling than that," Lineweber said. "I'm new at this, but I'm all in."

Anderson was quiet for a long time. Finally he said, "I do it for revenge, and I'm not new at it."

End of conversation.

At 8:30 p.m. in Girard, Illinois, Anderson and Lineweber waited. The prairie grass was swaying rhythmically as a warm breeze steadily rolled across the open prairie. It was black on the horizon, intermittently highlighted by flashes of heat lightning. Anderson and Lineweber solemnly sat in the pickup truck as the quiet little town folded up her streets. The sound of air conditioners hummed and distant thunder rumbled as darkness descended.

A white box truck displaying the Old Spaghetti House logo rolled into town on Route 4 and stopped at the four way stop sign. It was there for a long moment as the three occupants looked up and down the deserted streets. They made a left turn and headed west. Lineweber and Anderson followed them at a safe distance. Anderson used a handheld GPS to navigate to a location near the fertilizer storage shed, where they would park to walk across a bean field. The roads were dark and eerie flashes of light glistened on the soybean leaves like something ghostly materializing in the darkness.

They grabbed the M-16 rifles from behind the seat of the pickup truck; quickly attached silencers and started for the fertilizer shed. As they walked the lights from the box truck turned onto the dirt road and slowly headed down the lane. The wind increased and the thunder intensified. The bean field, plush and green, resembled the churning and heaving of ocean waves marching onto the beach as the wind howled. Lineweber watched the sky nervously, but Anderson s eyes were glued to the truck lights in the distance.

When the truck reached the shed Anderson and the Lineweber were no more than a hundred yards out, Anderson checked his clip and shucked a round into the chamber. Anyone who had ever been in combat would know the sound of an M-16 being locked and loaded . At that point he wasn't worried about being heard or seen. He was about to bring hellfire down on some demonic monsters and it wouldn't matter if they knew he was coming. They were already dead meat.

Lineweber tapped Anderson, on the shoulder. "I probably should have told you this before now, but I've never killed a man," he said quietly.

"Don't worry about it. I've killed enough of them for both of us," Anderson said softly.

Enormous lightning bolts electrified the sky, and the rumble of thunder was pulsating like a drum. They stood there for a moment before Anderson marched on.

"You don't have to fire a shot, just watch my back," Anderson said.

"You got it. I will." Lineweber said.

The driver of the box truck stepped out of the truck with a bolt cutter in his hand.

The other two occupants hopped out of the passenger seat. One of them was holding a flashlight and the other putting on work gloves. When Anderson came around the building the sky was white with light and his frame cast a huge shadow like an ancient Grecian god preparing to mete out justice. His teeth were clenched, his brow furrowed, eyes glared with hatred. Flashes from the M-16 dropped the first man as hot led tore through his chest. The others were so shocked they were frozen in their tracks. Their eyes wide, their skin pale in the black light of the night like two phantoms standing on their own graves. Fear was manifest on their faces. Death was eminent. Anderson emptied what was left of the 14 rounds in his clip, ejected the cartridge and shoved in another. They were both dead before they hit the ground. Lineweber stood as rigid as a stone, in awe.

When it was over a curtain of rain descended as the Grim Reaper tallied the dead martyrs sprawled upon the ground. In a few moments water was ankle deep, red with blood. Anderson gathered the bodies, hoisting them into the truck into a pile and slammed the overhead door. He said goodbye to Linweber and disappeared as the red taillights of the box truck vanished into the night.

Chapter Ten

St. Louis Metro East has a million people on the Illinois side of the Mississippi River. The cities of Venice, Madison and Sauget are littered with junk cars and empty rundown houses. Stray dogs are as plentiful as non-functioning traffic control lights on the pothole laden streets. In East St. Louis brush and saplings grow on top of abandoned multi-story building so abundantly that they resemble tiny rain forest in the sky. The poverty in the western portion of Metro East stretches from the Mississippi to State Route 157, where it abruptly ends. At that point the river valley meets a hillside where a societal upgrade becomes evident. The cities on the hillside are Edwardsville, Maryville, Belleville, Collinsville and a variety of other 'villes, that comprise the more prosperous portion of the urban sprawl. It's as though the poor and downtrodden were cascaded downward to reside in the low ground leaving the gainfully employed perched above them thanking God they didn't live west of 157.

The differences between them was stark, but there was a common thread subtly woven among them. It seemed that every hotel, convenient mart, and gas station was owned or operated by someone from an Arabian country. They prayed to the east at sunset, the woman covered their heads while in public, and they generally adhered to Sharia Law.

Anderson Claypool knew their sympathies and realized that if changes weren't made in US policies, this wouldn't be his last visit to the area, providing he survived. It was 2:30 a.m., and he was parked at St. Louis Ave., and Collinsville Rd. Bashaar Amir's brother and two hotel clerks were stacked in the enclosed truck bed resting in eternal peace.

The Bloody Onion Tavern was just down the hill on a parallel street within Anderson's view. The neon light in the window went dark as the last dogs sauntered to their cars. When they left the area it became as quiet as a cemetery. Bashaar's motel was two blocks west just across Route 157. It had originally been a Drury Inn, then Holiday Inn, Motel Six, Friendly Motel, and finally Bashaar's home. The tenants were wayward construction workers and down-and-outers who rented by the month. The swimming pool was empty, with yellow tape strung around it to keep inebriated guest from falling to their deaths. The parking lot was full of utility vans and rusty pickup trucks. On weekends it wasn't unusual for groups to be sitting on their tailgates drinking beer until the early morning hours, but it was Thursday and a workday was usually uneventful.

Anderson drove down the hillside and into the parking lot. He stopped in the rear where it was dark. He backed the truck between two U-Haul vans, stepped out and proceeded around to the front lobby. Bashaar was sitting in a leather chair behind the counter asleep. He was fully clothed; his cell phone on a table beside him. There was a counter and glass sliding window between them. Bashaar bolted out of his chair when

Anderson tapped the bell for service. His eyes were glazed and angry. It was clear he had been sitting there expecting something that should have already come about. Anderson knew what it was, but it wasn't going to happen. He was waiting for a call from his brother Ahmed to assess him on the ammonium nitrate run.

Bashaar slid the window open and irritatedly said, "No rooms."

Anderson had taken Bashaar's brother's cell phone and programmed it to ring Bashaar's number. He reached inside his pocket and depressed a button. At that moment Bashaar's phone rang. "Excuse me," he said. He hurried to grab the phone, turned his back and stepped behind a partition. Anderson shoulders were too wide to fit the narrow passageway that had been left open so he turned his body sideways and propelled himself through the window with the agility of an Olympic gymnast. He could hear Bashaar repeating "hello," several times in English, and finally in Arabic. When he turned around Anderson was standing over him. Shock and fear flashed across his face as he lurched away. Anderson grabbed the back of his neck and pulled him forward. He inserted a knife blade between his ribs just deep enough to break the skin. He stared into Bashaar's eyes for a second just to witness the epiphany contained within them, the knowledge that he was going to die. He pushed the blade slowly in, making sure it punctured Bashaar's heart. He twisted the handle and watched as the light faded from his gaze.

Anderson left Bashaar lying in the hallway. He walked calmly to the rear bedroom in the living quarters. He cracked the door and saw and elderly Arab man sleeping there. He quietly approached the bed, slipped his hand behind the man's neck and raised him gently forward. The old man opened his eyes. Anderson said, "Allah Akbar," as he slid the knife across his throat.

At 5:30 a.m., Anderson exited I-55 at Sikeston, Missouri, just about two hours north of Memphis. The five bodies inside the box truck were lying haphazardly on the floor. Some of them had been roughed up from the long ride. Anderson knew they were thumping around as they slid from one side to the other knocking their heads and torsos against the van walls. It was heartwarming to have five terrorist riddled with bullet holes scuffed up from a postmortem misadventure: riding the sway like so many sacks of potatoes.

Anderson turned beneath the overpass and drove two miles to the Basler Funeral Home. Raymond Basler was waiting in the parking lot when Anderson arrived. He was wearing his usual charcoal colored suit, a white shirt and red tie. Basler was 64 years old, gray and as thin as a number two pencil. He didn't look like a soldier fighting the good fight against evil, but he was. When his son was killed in Afghanistan, he joined the struggle to mitigate the pain of his loss and to retaliate. He wasn't on the front lines slicing people's throats, and emptying fourteen round clips into them, but he performed an important function. He caused dead bodies to disappear.

Together Basler and Anderson loaded the dead bodies upon a flatbed gurney to transport them to their final resting place. On their way they passed three other deceased waiting their turns to plunge into the fire. They were legitimate customers, and their disposal was less urgent as they lie dressed in their fitted suits and dresses. The furnace was already jetting bright blue flames and in only moments five dead terrorists vanished into dust.

At eight thirty a.m., Anderson was dressed in his black suit sitting inside the security station at the Harmon Edison estate, as though nothing had happened. His computer screen was displaying the Belleville Democrat. There were two separate articles describing local St. Louis merto east deaths during the previous evening. One of them described how a popular Belleville physician died of a drug overdose. His closest friends in total shock and disbelief proclaimed that his drug use was such a secret that even they didn't know. In the other article, an Airman at Scott Air Force base had hanged himself. His friends confirmed he had been acting strange lately, but they never suspected he would commit suicide.

It had been a busy night for Anderson Claypool.

Chapter Eleven

The sun was setting behind the tree line in the distant Mississippi River bottoms. A young beautiful blue-eyed girl stood with folded arms as the humid breeze ferried in the faint sounds of music from downtown Memphis. Like a young woman in a vivid memory, her long brown hair was flowing on the wind and her smooth skin aglow in the dim evening light. She was living in the moment. Unlike those glowing moments of Morgan's youth, her moments were excruciatingly painful. Fear smoldered in her mind, and regret was her reality. The lonely cry of a whippoorwill echoing across the river bottoms was the defining cry of her existence. She wore sadness like a cloak. Happiness was a wasteland away.

She watched Anderson strolling on the sidewalk near the house with one hand in his pocket and a toothpick in his mouth. She was beginning to like Anderson. Maybe it was because he was so easy. He was supposed to guard her but sometimes he was so detached that she thought she might just climb unnoticed onto the fence and dive to her death down the cliffs to Riverside Drive. Anderson's eyes sometimes seemed to offer something that intrigued her, but she couldn't put her finger on it. He had only been with Edison for about a year but he seemed to know everything. He appeared to know that she wouldn't run. He knew she didn't have another place in the world to go. She had forgotten how to fight, how to survive. She hated it here with Harmon Edison, but somehow it was impossible to leave. She sensed that Anderson knew that and when he looked at her, his eyes said, "I get it."

Edison named her Sonya Isles. Her real name was Tara Carter. Edison said he wouldn't utter her real name because it was pure "white trash." Tara Carter would have been a smoker; her bad hair would have been rigid with hair spray, and a rose would have been tattooed on her thigh. Sonya was exotic and elegant, without defect or blemish. Sonya Isles was a fitting name for such a rare and subtle creature.

Sonya never attended school beyond the seventh grade, but with home schooling she graduated from high school, and with private professors she received a degree from the University of Memphis; all before her nineteenth birthday. A dentist visited her on a regular basis, and an M.D. frequented the home for routine physicals. She had a library at her disposal, and satellite TV was available in every room of the house. She didn't have a cell phone, nor access to a land line. She was allowed to go shopping as long as she was escorted by security staff, that being Anderson for the last year. Edison had chosen a few young ladies to come to his home as one might arrange play dates for a child. She had everything but, she had nothing. Still there was that feeble hope, but it was waning. Sonya's fleeting prayer was on the back of Jose Garcia.

Jose was a wanted man. There were wanted posters out all over the country for his apprehension and a hefty reward for his return. There were people like Morgan and Rudy, legitimate and legal, searching for him, but Sonya feared there were others too.

Sonya had given him a treasure for safe-keeping before he left. That was what Edison wanted. He had offered a $20,000 reward for Jose, but he would have easily paid $200,000.

Sonya feared that Edison's money would, in the end, dash her hopes.

Sonya was born outside West Memphis in a rundown trailer house at the edge of a cotton field, the yard cluttered with junk cars, broken down appliances, and worn out tires. Stray dogs had worn down the grass and the dirt around the house was as hard as concrete. Her father was killed in an armed robbery attempt in Cape Girardeau, Missouri when she was seven years old. His legacy was embossed in her memory but she couldn't remember his face.

Sonya was thirteen when she and her mother moved to a rooming house at 5300 Telegraph Street in Memphis. Sonya's mother took in nightly visitors who sometimes became weekly or monthly guests. One of them found Sonya on the couch one night when her mother was passed out drunk. She didn't know if she was raped, or if her lack of resistance equaled consent. She understood what was happening. She knew her mother had done it hundreds of times for money. It was awful for her. It was painful and degrading, but she didn't know for sure that she was raped. She didn't fight it, she just laid there trying desperately to think of something pleasant to distract her and prayed for it to be over. Was that rape?

Before she was fourteen her belly was bulging,

and she was suffering morning sickness. She had stopped going to school. She spent her days sitting in the dark dingy room with clutter building around her until one morning she found her mother dead in the bathroom with a needle in her arm. When the police came to investigate, they took Sonya and deposited her at Edison House For Girls.

Now Sonya was living with Edison. She was taken from Edison House by Edison himself, and declared a special case. There were many special cases and circumstances surrounding Edison House that were suspicious, but who could argue with the improvements Harmon Edison's generosity offered? By any normal measurement, her life was infinitely better than it had been before Edison plucked her from the depths of despair. Now she was educated, well-groomed, and the results of good nutrition and physical well-being were evident in her hair and skin. She was as beautiful as any young woman in Memphis, maybe the entire state of Tennessee.

To be born into hopelessness is often mitigated by the half knowledge of despair. People who suffer the indignation of poverty from birth will accept it and confront its ills, but they can't comprehend what resides on the other side. That's the buffer protecting them from reality. They understand the tyranny of being dirt poor, but those who reside beyond it are the infamous "they." Victims like Tara Carter see the world as a place full of "theys." It was a different world where "they" live. To reside in desperation, and yet have knowledge of the other is the cruelest fate. Half knowledge of despair is no blessing. Sonya Isles crossed over to the other side; she was an old soul. She had seen the world from both sides. Despair is a hungry dog who steals a piece of meat but is beaten down and relieved of his cache before he can swallow it. He's left with the taste in his mouth and an empty ache in his stomach.

There were terrible things going on in Sonya's world but she felt helpless to change them. She was intelligent, educated, and healthy, but her soul was still in the other world. She knew awful things were happening in Edison House for Girls - things that were unspeakable but she didn't do anything to stop them. She still had the mentality of Tara Carter. She fully recognized despair but was helpless to do anything about it and therein was the source of her misery.

Chapter Twelve

It was eight-thirty as Morgan and Rudy arrived in Fort Lauderdale. It was dark but the sky was washed in a vanilla glow from the city lights. People strolled on the beach and flashlight beams crisscrossed in the dark as tourist searched for sand crabs. Rudy rolled down the windows and let the warm evening breeze flow through the car. Hotels and restaurants with manicured lawns, and stylish landscaping were prominent on one side of Route A1-A Boulevard, and a newly-constructed retaining wall separated the roadway from the beach. Fort Lauderdale's tall stately palms occupied the sand between the roadway and the ocean, a tropical paradise. On quiet nights the palm leaves rustle in the breeze, and people lie on blankets in the dark watching the stars.

Fort Lauderdale was beautiful and exciting and even though their visit was not a vacation, its appeal was not lost. They were there to find and apprehend Jose Garcia. The mysterious Jesus character said he would be in the Nets End Tavern in the evening at about 6:30. Although Hollywood was only a short distance from Fort Lauderdale, the window for finding the tavern was closing, so they decided to check into a hotel and call it a day.

They tried a variety of hotels but without

reservations they were turned back again and again. In an act of desperation they settled for the Sea Breeze Inn. It was located right on the beach near the boardwalk, a stone's throw from the ocean. As far as locations go, it couldn't have been better, but its clientele was less than desirable. Most of the windows were open with wet towels hanging out of them in the evening air to dry. Fat men grilled hot dogs and hamburgers on Smoky Joes on the balconies as women in two piece bathing suits climbed through the windows in lieu of using the doors. Pedro and Maria were right at home as they visited with other Mexicans who freely shared their Modelo while keeping beat to raucous Latino music. Morgan made his required call to Anderson. It was a short conversation. Anderson asked if there was anything new, and Morgan advised that they had only just arrived. Anderson said, "Okay," and that was it.

Yellow and red lights from restaurants and bars were glowing while girls donning roller blades zipped along the boardwalk. The beach was dark and only the white caps on the waves were visible in the dark water. Italian restaurants were busy selling pizza by the slice as customers meandered from one beach-side bar to the next refilling plastic cups with beer. There was a small amphitheater just off the boardwalk between two eucalyptus trees where Rudy had taken off his shoes and socks, rolled up his pant legs and sat dangling his legs off the stage. It was sure good to be Rudy Campbell. Morgan took off his shoes and sauntered around in the sand as the Latino music drifted along on the breeze. It wasn't bad to be Morgan Cooper either. Morgan hit the sack early while Rudy, Pedro and Maria talked with a group of young Hispanics late into the night. Morgan dreamed of Molly.

The bright sunlight was ablaze around the window curtains when Morgan opened his eyes. He had fallen into a new sleeping pattern. When he was back in Willoughby Hills he never slept past 6:30 a.m., but now 6:30 seemed early. Rudy was already up wandering the hallways and talking to anyone who would engage in a conversation. He was dressed in his new green polo shirt, Tommy jeans, and new soft leather loafers. Morgan stepped onto the balcony. Rudy came through the window with two hot cups of coffee, grunting as he heisted his leg over the windowsill. Morgan chuckled under his breath, "When in Rome."

They sipped on their coffee and discussed how they would handle the Pedro/Maria situation. They were still broke and homeless, but there were many Mexican families there in Hollywood who could help them out. Morgan thought he might be able to tide them over with some cash from the expense money. Once they finished their investigation Edison could deduct it from their fee. They agreed, but Rudy seemed a little let down. He wondered aloud what might happen if the police stumbled onto them. Still the deal was done. They would be saying goodbye

It was eleven a.m. before Morgan was checked out. Pedro and Maria's faces were drawn and their sad eyes had an expression of impending doom. They looked like two people who were entering the abode of the damned. Their association had not yet spanned four days, but their friendship was amalgamated in battle, baptized in blood. They had traveled through several states, eaten their meals, and stunk up the car together.

It now seemed like a way of life.

Pedro's gloom departed the arena when Morgan handed him five one-hundred dollar bills, which would help to mitigate the pain of separation. Maria grabbed at it but Pedro was too quick for her and soon the deniero was in his pocket. Pedro was headed off to who knows where, and Maria was on his heels. As an afterthought she flashed a smile and said in English, "Goodbye, my friends."

Morgan and Rudy were off to locate the Nets End Tavern. They drove to the west side of Hollywood where they found a neighborhood with brightly-colored green, yellow and orange, ranch style houses. There were restaurants and bars with Spanish advertisements plastered on the windows. The Nets End Tavern was located on a corner lot in a building that had once been a residence. A rectangular addition had been added to the original structure and the back yard transformed into a parking lot. A wrecked fishing boat draped with fish net was tilted on its side and a sign with faded block letters identified the place as The Net's End Tavern. A newer homemade Spanish version was attached to a stake in the ground.

It was still early so they drove around familiarizing themselves with the neighborhood. It was only 4:30 p.m., and according to The Jesus, Jose wouldn't be there for a few hours. If they found Jose, would they simply grab him and take him into custody? Did they even have authority to apprehend him? They left the neighborhood and found a more upscale part of town with a Holiday Inn. A sign in the reception area indicated that it was Wi-Fi-equipped. Morgan broke out the laptop and pulled up the web. Florida laws prohibited bounty hunting, but they had a reciprocal agreement with Illinois regarding licensed Private Investigators. Whatever laws private detectives were allowed to enforce in Illinois, they were also allowed to enforce in Florida. Morgan researched the Florida Private Detective Act on the computer while Rudy looked over his shoulder.

"We can conduct investigations, we can follow him covertly, or even overtly without fear of being arrested for stalking. We can question him, and finally we can apprehend him and hold him if there is a reasonable certainty that he's committed a felony, or if he's wanted by law enforcement authorities."

"Then we're good to go," Rudy said.

"We're good to go."

With that being the situation, they drove back to the neighborhood and took a position a few blocks from the Net's End. As they waited for time to pass, rusty vans and pickup trucks dropped off Latino men who were covered with drywall dust and paint, carrying empty lunch pails and toolboxes which they later deposited outside the back entrance. They stopped on the sidewalks in groups and talked. Little Mexican kids ran through the yards and rode their skateboards down the broken sidewalks. They waved goodbye to each other as they disappeared inside their homes. It all seemed so extraordinarily normal.

Rudy was silent. Morgan studied him, wondering what might be going through his mind. He knew that Rudy was a red -blooded American from his head to his feet. Whenever there was a gray line, he usually found a way of reducing it to something concrete, then he took a side. Now it was evident that something had changed. His experience with Pedro and Maria had softened his views.

"You know, Morgan, they need to change some of these immigration laws. It ain't right for people like Pedro and Maria to be criminals just because they want to make a living."

Morgan agreed. Mexicans and Latinos were risking their lives to come to the States to take jobs Americans wouldn't do. It was hard enough to pry some people off the couch to go to the welfare office, much less to go to work. Latinos crossed the Gulf of Mexico on make-shift rafts and marched across the desert just to get a job. For Morgan, it was hard to resent people who were hard working and family-oriented. The Latinos he knew fit into that category. But still it wasn't good just to open the borders and let people flock in by the thousands. It wasn't a good thing for Americans or the illegal immigrants. Illegal immigration was ravaging the State of Arizona, but most people didn't have a clue. The borders were a long way from most of America.

Both Morgan and Rudy were quietly pondering the reality of being involved in it firsthand when they saw several young Mexicans crammed into a white Chevy Van turning into the Nets End parking lot. Rudy grabbed for his wanted poster as he eyeballed the six or seven men who got out of the van and went inside by the rear entrance. Several other people entered at the front door. They were too far away to get a good view of their faces, and the wanted poster was so worn out that identifying someone from it would be impossible.

It was already six-fifteen, so they drove to the parking lot and went into the bar. It was the typical dimly-lit, smoke filled, crammed up hole in the wall. A few whites were seated at the bar, but the crowd was overwhelmingly Hispanic. Corona and Modelo signs decorated the walls and low slung banners. A Latino song was playing on the jukebox as an older couple danced in an open area where the chairs had been pushed aside. In the very back a group of men varying in age from 20 to 40, were gathered around two tables that had been joined together. One man had taken off his boots and left them on the floor.

As Morgan and Rudy scanned the room, Morgan saw something that caused him to smile. In a dark corner under a blinking Budweiser sign, Pedro and Maria were sitting at a table with several empty glasses in front of them. Maria was having a Margarita and Pedro was enjoying bourbon on the rocks. Morgan rolled his eyes and gave a head nod in their direction. Rudy laughed. "I guess cold beer wasn't good enough for them." Rudy chuckled.

"It's good to see our money's not being wasted on commodities like food and shelter." Morgan said.

They both shook their heads in disbelief as they found stools at the bar. How in hell did they get there, and what were the chances they would show up in the very same place as Morgan and Rudy? Would the wonders never cease?

It was a momentary distraction. Rudy went back to analyzing the faces in the rear corner of the tavern. A man about 35 to 40 with long brown hair resembled the face on the poster.

"Is that him?" Rudy asked.

"That good looking kid?"

"Yeah, but he ain't a kid, Morgan. He's middle-aged."

"I can't tell. Everybody looks like a kid to me these days," Morgan said.

The men at the table were noticeably quieter than they had been earlier. A few quick glances in Morgan and Rudy's direction from one of the men might have signaled that they were suspicious, but they took turns peeking around a post, and occasionally one of them might lean his head into a friend's shoulder and whisper. It wasn't hard to see that they were sizing them up. In a place like that when a cop was in the room everybody knew it. It didn't make a difference that they were old -- they might as well have had a sign posted on their backs. "Here we are a couple of old cops looking for a pinch."

Rudy slid off his stool and leaned his shoulder into a supporting beam between himself the table of men. One of them got up and walked past Rudy, headed for the restroom. Rudy sipped on his beer. Morgan watched the group by way of the mirror behind the bar.

When the man came out of the restroom Rudy was looking around the beam when he was jolted from behind. Beer spilled onto the floor, and Rudy spun around off balance. He had been bumped hard.

"Cual es su problemo, chingala!" the man said in a growl.

Morgan was off his stool in an instant and stood between them.

"No habla Espanol, Amigo," he said.

The other men were out of their chairs and closing in on them. One of his buddies leaned forward. "He don't speak no Englese, but he said, 'what's your problem?'

Rudy popped out his badge and held it at eye level. "We're look'n for somebody. We're not here for trouble."

Rudy could have been the poster boy for men who overextend their authority. Just the fact that he was in Florida, and not Illinois, left him without legal jurisdiction, but in addition to that he was also retired. Yet there he stood with his retired officers badge dangling in the air with disdain shining behind his two black eyes.

The man came closer. With narrowed eyes he strained to inspect Rudy's badge. "You're retired. That means you're not a real cop, Amigo."

"Wrong, my friend, since 911, all retired cops have been reactivated."

Morgan swallowed hard and fished for his private detective badge. At least there was a reciprocal agreement between Florida and Illinois. The last thing he wanted was to be arrested for impersonating a police officer. He didn't have it. It was in his suitcase.

The man edged just a little closer, eyeballing the monogram on Rudy's shirt. He smiled. "You must be the Memphis Zoo Police." He turned around and grinned at the others. "Es possible que el sea del zoologico de la policia!"

The place went up in laughter.

"Maybe you're the raccoon police," he said, looking at Rudy's black eyes.

"You need to back off," Rudy warned.

"This isn't gonna be more of that real detective work, is it, Rudy?"

So far a thorough beating had been incorporated into their investigative routine. It seemed like things were headed south right at that moment. And then from the darkened recesses of the tavern Pedro and Maria stepped up. Pedro was still wearing his Nilly Vanilly t-shirt, Maria her embroidered jeans. Maria ran and hugged Morgan. Pedro shouted, "Amigos, Rudy e Morgan!" He grabbed Rudy's hand and shook it like he hadn't seen him for ten years. They were completely overcome by their unexpected meeting.

At that point they took over the negotiations between Morgan, Rudy and the Mexicans. In Spanish they explained that they were great friends, and that Morgan and Rudy were splendid fellows. Maria's hands were making a circling motion in the air as she explained wide-eyed how their trailer was sucked into a cloud, and then she huddled as though she was going to crawl under the table. Pedro hugged Rudy and pulled his neck into his shoulders as he demonstrated in a crouched position how they had huddled under the bridge together. Maria took over again, picking up a chair to show the Mexicans how she shoved the chair behind Jimmy's legs, then Pedro's fist were punching the air illustrating how he beat on Jimmy's head.

The Mexicans were laughing, hanging on Pedro and Maria's every word. Morgan and Rudy smiled, not understanding the words, but the animation was easy to read and they were able to follow the story.

Maria was so excited that she interrupted Pedro as he was trying to show how Jimmy's head was bouncing as he punched it. Maria was jabbering with spit spewing into the air. She reached onto a table and found a fork, then raised it high into the air and then pretended to plunge it into Jimmy's chest, explaining how she had stuck him. The Mexicans watched in astonishment. Maria pointed at Rudy as she explained how Rudy had told them to scram, then she shouted, "Vamoose!" Pedro turned his cap backwards and ran in place as he pretended to head for the door. The Mexicans laughed and slapped him on the back. A few of them shook Rudy and Morgan's hand as they moseyed back to their chairs.

Without being able to communicate, the four friends stood there looking at each other affectionately. "Unbelievable," Rudy snorted. Pedro shrugged.

Maria pointed towards the back of the tavern. "Jose Garcia," she said.

Morgan looked at her. "What?"

Maria pointed again, "Jose Garcia."

The handsome Mexican was leaving by the back door. "Oh, man! I forgot what we were doing here," Morgan exclaimed.

Without debating their course of action they went for the front door and ran to Rudy's car. A 1978 Oldsmobile was leaving the rear parking lot spraying gravel from the back tires. Rudy slammed the car into gear but stopped when he heard screaming. Pedro and Maria were both trying to climb into the back seat as the car rolled to a stop.

"What the hell!"

"You guys are just like two little dogs," Morgan said as he reached across the back seat and jerked Maria into the car.

"Gracias!"

The Olds was rounding the corner with the tires squealing with blue smoke streaming from the tailpipe. Rudy punched it! Pedro and Maria were slammed against the back seat. Another car was approaching the intersection but Rudy rammed through. The Olds' taillights were several blocks ahead of them and gaining speed. The Olds caught the green light at the intersection, but it was amber long before Rudy got there. It turned red!

"Don't do it, Rudy!"

Rudy hit the brakes, hesitated for an instant, then floored it. They shot through the intersection with other cars weaving to miss them. Brakes were screeching, horns blaring and middle fingers raised in angry protests. Maria was screaming and Pedro cupped his hands over his eyes.

"Jesus Christ, Rudy, that was stupid!"

In that split second Rudy was cast across the passage of time. He wasn't a retired cop now. He was in his squad car in hot pursuit, cramming it. His red and blue lights were flashing and his siren wailing. A high speed pursuit was in progress. Rudy's adrenaline was powering through his veins and reality was gone with the wind.

"Rudy, stop!"

The Olds turned a corner ahead of them just as a car crossed the road from a side street. Rudy swerved, the tires squealed, the Lincoln slid sideways and fishtailed into oncoming traffic. Rudy fought the steering wheel wildly as it swapped ends and humped onto the sidewalk! Pedro and Maria sat stunned, but thankful to be alive. Morgan jumped out of the car and slammed the door. "Rudy, you stupid moron! Rudy silently held onto the steering wheel. The air had been let out of him, and the realization of what he had done was sinking in. "Morgan, I'm sorry. I don't know what got into me. I lost it."

"You got that right. Hell, you could have killed somebody. Hell, you could've killed a little kid, or the frick'n Pope if he was here!"

"Get in the car, Morgan. I'm sorry."

"I'm out of here, I'm going home!"

"Come on Morgan, you can't go home. Get in."

Morgan stomped around with his hands in his pockets. Rudy sat behind the steering wheel for a moment, then backed off the sidewalk and parked alongside the curb. Pedro got out while Maria waited in the back seat. He walked across the street to a corner restaurant and came back with four cups of coffee.

Rudy relieved Pedro of two cups and extended his hand to Morgan to take one of them. Morgan rolled his eyes and avoided the offer but Rudy was persistent. "Come on Morgan, Pedro was kind enough to buy coffee with our money. We can't be insensitive, can we?"

Morgan accepted the coffee and shook his head as he bit his lower lip. "If you pull another stunt like that we're through, understand?"

"I do, Morgan. I'll drive like your grandma from now on."

Chapter Thirteen

A long black limo stopped in front of Edison House. Anderson and a young Arab in a blue suit stepped out onto the sidewalk. An elderly woman waited at the side gate to the entrance while Anderson and his companion crossed the sidewalk and hurried down the cobblestone path to the door and went inside. A moment later they returned with two attractive girls who looked to be about 15 years old. Anderson opened the limo door and ushered them inside. Another older Arab was sitting with Harmon Edison. He leered at the girls seated across from him. He held two pictures in his hand, alternating his glances from the photos to the girls. The Arab appeared to be in his early sixties and wore a black and white checkered keffiyeh, a thonbe and bisht. The thonbe was faint green and the bisht was sheer white silk. In the Arab world those robes were supposed to be a symbol of modesty, but there was nothing modest about this lecherous demon. He leaned forward and reached across the opposing seat and took one of the girls by her hand. She rose from her seat following along as she was pulled across the car. He helped her into the seat next to him. She was bewildered and confused, but a lifetime served in the throes of despair had conditioned her to accept what "they" were doing to her. He placed his arm around her shoulder and pulled her close to him. He held onto her hand as he guided it beneath his robe. The girl trembled and her lip quivered, but she didn't resist. The man's lips curled into an evil grin. He momentarily glanced at Edison before shifting a blank stare out the window. He released the girl's hand and pushed her back across the car. "Very good," he said arrogantly.

He picked up his laptop and opened it to an offshore account. He pushed the send button and a deposit was made to Harmon Edison for $500,000. Edison shook his hand. "It's nice doing business with you, Mr. Abib." The limo door opened and Edison stepped out. Anderson was waiting for him in the Lincoln Town Car. The limo turned onto Union St. and disappeared around the corner.

Sonya Isles was in her third story bedroom looking out across the Mississippi River. She could see into Arkansas far beyond West Memphis, past the lights and into the darkness of the Delta. She thought about her trailer home at the edge of the cotton field. She wondered why she and her mother didn't clean up the tires and junk around the house and maybe plant some grass and flowers in the yard. Why didn't her mom find a job working in an office or a factory? Sonya knew now that she was capable of learning. She was a college graduate after all. She could have gone to public school and earned a scholarship. She and her mom could have saved their money and bought a better house. They could have taken better care of themselves and kept themselves clean. She was doing that now. She knew the importance of oral hygiene and a good diet. They didn't have to be rich to do those things. She could have met a nice boy who lived on a farm and worked with his dad planting the fields and tending to the cattle. She could have lived a normal life. Her memory of her mother was bittersweet vacillating between resenting her for giving up on life so early and pitying her for never knowing there was another way.

They were so close to being normal, yet worlds away. Fresh breath, clean skin and hair, and a little hard work will lift you from the depths of despair. It was so simple. Sometimes just being presentable and living in a clean house can elevate a

person to respectability. Money wasn't the determining factor. She had money now. She had everything a person could want, but her respectability still eluded her. To believe that she had lost something in her transformation was absurd. Her life before Harmon Edison was a dead end. If she had been lucky enough to survive she would most likely be living on the street or worse. Yet she envisioned a parallel world where she was wholesome and happy in a place that might have been.

Harmon Edison loved Sonya but he had never touched her. He adored her in a peculiar and eccentric way. Sonya was beautiful even without being polished but Edison had refined her and contributed to her development so profoundly that he thought of himself as an artist with her as his canvass. He would never have touched her in a sexual way. Since Sonya had come into his life she had totally consumed him. She was a distraction from the scurrilous life he had garnered. To soil her would be no less than a travesty. No one else would ever touch her either. She wasn't on the market and never would be.

Being the object of Edison's affection and desire wasn't what Sonya wanted. She wanted her freedom but she didn't know how to find her way to it. She believed she would forever be a prisoner but she was wrong. Help was advancing in her direction at that very moment. Something small but so significant was about to turn things upside down. Information is power. Information was the only thing Sonya didn't have at her disposal, but that was about to change. Anderson was walking silently down the hallway towards her room. He slowly opened her door and looked inside. She was startled, but privacy didn't exist in her world, so she quickly recovered.

"What is it, Anderson?"

"We need to talk, Miss Sonya." His expression was strange, his voice lower, his accent gone. He held a laptop computer in his hand. Sonya had never been permitted to use a computer. Technology didn't exist for her.

"If I may sit with you, I'll show you something you need to know." Anderson said.

At that point Anderson proceeded to show Sonya the basics, starting with how to turn it on. There was a lot to learn, but she was a quick study. Anderson knew computers, had a patience about him, a good teacher. He explained that she had access to a bank account, credit cards, and travel information. She was astounded to find that airline tickets, car rentals and hotels could be obtained with a click of a button on the internet. Anderson quietly and systematically began to give her a power she previously had not known to exist. After an hour Anderson left her alone with her computer.

A captive soul was about to be freed.

Back in Hollywood, Florida, Morgan and Rudy were driving through the Hispanic district slowly searching for the 1978 Oldsmobile. Pedro and Maria were returned to The Net's End to resume wasting the $500 stake Morgan had given them. It was after nine and they had been looking for Jose for more than three hours. They didn't want to give up but their chances were diminishing as the night wore on. Finally Rudy turned onto a pothole-laden boulevard lined with squatty, yellowed palms. In the middle of the block there was a decrepit motel, the kind of place where construction workers flop when working on site away from home. This was a home for illegal immigrants. Mexicans were lined against the walls sitting in plastic chairs that most likely had come from a laundromat somewhere. A handmade sign dangling from a steel post identified it as the Paradise Motel. Behind it was a parking lot that had once been asphalt but had now deteriorated to a mixture of gravel and black clumps of pavement. Sparks and smoke rose into the air from the burn barrel planted in the middle of the parking lot, while men with Budweiser cans in their fists milled about. In the darkest parking area of the lot they spotted the Olds. Rudy guided his car into the space next to it.

"That's it, Morgan."

Morgan agreed. There were only a few of those big boats still around. Being old-timers, they had seen their share of them through the years. They both knew a '78 Olds when they saw it.

Most of the motel doors were standing open displaying worn, shoddy furniture and dirty unmade beds. Curious residents were beginning to take an interest in the newcomers as Morgan stepped out of the car and visually inspected the Olds. Little kids stood silently watching them. Moments passed as the adults began to abandon their plastic chairs and their positions around the burn barrel to join the children.

"Cui Pasa, Senor?" one man asked in an inquisitive tone.

"We're looking for somebody," Morgan said.

An older thin but shapely woman approached them cautiously but with deliberate intent. Her healthy salt and pepper hair was pulled back in a neat bun. Intuitive deep brown eyes revealed a lifetime of struggle and pain, but it had not diminished her beauty. There were others who followed her, ready to come to her aid. She was clearly highly respected among them. She introduced herself as Angelique Sanchez.

"The car, it is my son's. Why are you looking at it?"

The conversation started in a cat and mouse fashion as most field inquiries do. Neither party wanted to give up too much information, but little bits had to be provided to elicit additional conversation. Both Morgan and Rudy had been patrolmen for the entirety of their careers, and they had never learned the art of deception. Lying for information had never been a technique for either of them, and Morgan wasn't going to start now. He would tell her who he was and why they were there. If she closed down, then so be it.

"Your son would be Jose Garcia?" Morgan asked.

"Yes, a good son. A son I'm very proud of."

"He's a wanted man. They say he burglarized a

home in Memphis, Tennessee. The homeowner made a police report, and there's a reward for his arrest. We're contracted by the owner to facilitate his return for trial."

"You're bounty hunters, then?"

"No, we're retired police officers. It's a case for us. I'm a licensed private detective. It's what we do."

"You hunt down innocent men for rich people. I don't see any difference," Angelique said coolly.

"He's a criminal and an illegal immigrant," Rudy butted in.

"He is not an illegal immigrant. My son is an American citizen."

"The wanted poster says different," Rudy spouted.

"There's a story behind all of this, but if you're only interested in grabbing my son and hauling him back to Memphis without even listening to the truth, then get back in your car and go find him wherever you can!"

Several onlookers with determined expressions were ready to pounce if necessary.

"We'll listen," Morgan said.

That was good enough to ease the tension. Two men fetched wood from a metal box at the end of the parking lot. They transferred fire from the burn barrel to the wood pile. Chairs were gathered from where they had been lined against the wall and placed in a circle around the fire. It was as though they were preparing for a theatrical event. The men and women were friendly and helpful. Beer coolers were carried from the rooms. Rudy accepted a beer when it was offered, but Morgan declined. It was hard enough to stay focused without having beer goggles on.

When the Mexicans saw that their visitors were willing to listen, their hearts were opened. They treated them as honored guests. It was pitiful to watch. They were facing peril from authority, pure disdain from most Americans, but their response was trust and benevolence. The animosity had not jaded them or made them bitter. They were living in an underworld where life beyond the parking lot of the motel was a world away. They walked to the corner grocers for their food, and they gathered together in the evenings drinking beer and hoping the police didn't have a reason to stop and question them. They worked for peanuts and still had enough money to send back home. When a squad car cruised by the men would slowly split for their dingy rooms, knowing that if they hurried it might look like they were getting ready to run. Whenever a Mexican was caught running it was cause for investigation.

Morgan and Rudy weren't dispensing hope, but they were willingness to listen, for the Mexicans it was indemnity from their drudgery. "They will help," was the message in their eyes.

The flame from the fire caused shadows to dance across the parking lot and flicker on the motel walls. Angelique sat in her chair looking into the light. Her features were delicate and the warm glow of the firelight softened the wrinkles around her eyes. She was an elegant woman. She merited more than had been bestowed upon her, but she was so well founded that she endured it with dignity and grace. She was wearing a long charcoal-colored dress with gray buttons. It was svelte and covered her from the collar to her ankles. She would have been as appropriately seated at the hearth of a classic southern mansion as she was there at the fire, and no less at home.

Her story began in the mountains south of Le lectyra, Mexico in the late forties. Her parents were Jorge Garcia, and Marguerite Sanchez. Jorge was 30, and Marguerite was twenty four. Each year they left their village and traveled north to the United States. In those days nobody complained about illegal immigration or even paid attention to the Hispanics who came to America to work. Angeliques's parents picked oranges in Florida, peaches in Georgia, cotton in Mississippi, and pumpkins in Illinois and Indiana. When the crops were harvested, they went home for the winter.

Angelique was born in Osceola, Arkansas on December 24th, 1953 on the Martin McCabe cotton farm. She was delivered by a black farm hand in the loft of McCabe's barn. She was an American citizen, but she didn't have a birth certificate. She was born here and didn't leave the country until she was seventeen years old.

Angelique didn't remember the early years she spent in the Midwest. She knew that after she was born her parents decided to stay in the US permanently, moving around from one town to another working where they could. Citizenship wasn't a concern. Everybody knew they were from Mexico, but it wasn't important. They hated the cold weather and frequently talked about going back home, but poverty was waiting for them there. It was the kind of poverty Americans wouldn't be able to understand. It was a place without medicine, or running water, a place where children played in filth, and starvation was rampant. Jorge and Marguerite were considered poor in America but being poor here was abundantly better than being poor in Mexico. With that as their motivation, they stayed.

In the late 1950's Jorge packed everything they owned into his 1949 Dodge pickup truck and struck out for California. He found work at the August Triano winery in the upper Napa Valley region. He worked in the vineyard, and Marguerite worked as a housemaid and cook in the home of August Triano. They commuted daily from -Pasadena to the winery. When Jorge proved to be a hard working dependable employee, August moved them to a small cottage on the property. August Triano was 59 at that time. Angelique was eleven.

Angelique described her home in California as the most beautiful place on earth. She said the house was made of cobblestone and brick and adorned with ivy. The grape vines were so close to the cottage that she could pick them from her bedroom window. In the autumn the vineyard was often blanketed by a morning haze, and when the sun rose over the mountains it washed everything with an amber glow so splendid it was like gazing into heaven.

When Angelique was seventeen, August Triano was sixty-five. He had a daughter, 41-year-old Rosa. She was his only child. August was a kind and gentle man, but Rosa didn't have those same qualities. She was as strong and hard as a hickory tree, and as mean as Lucifer himself. August knew grapes better than anyone in the valley, and his wine was known throughout the world. When August's wife died in 1966, Rosa became the business manager. Together

August and Rosa governed one of the most successful winery in California.

Angelique paused for a moment and watched the growing fire. Her entourage sat quietly with their eyes lowered in solemn respect for her. They knew the next phase of the story; they had heard it before and knew it was painful for her.

"August loved two things," Angelique said quietly. Her eyes welled with tears. Time had not robbed her of her beauty, and it had not diminished her pain.

"He loved making wine, and he loved me."

Morgan studied her features, and Rudy put his chin in his hand and watched her absorbed by her tale Her voice was so soft and calming - almost melodic. Her Mexican accent was diminished, but still evident enough to be captivating.

Seventeen year old Angelique and the elderly August became lovers. She painfully acknowledged the stigma of an old man seducing a girl a third his age, but she proclaimed her love for him was real and defied anyone to argue that his love for her wasn't sincere. They were not open with the affair, but everyone suspected it. Rosa despised her and openly harassed her. When Angelique became pregnant, it was all out war between them.

Jose Garcia was born on November 12, 1970, but that wasn't his given name. His birth certificate identified him as Antonio Triano, and his father as August Triano. Jose Garcia was, in fact, the son of one of America's richest citizens.

"It is astonishing, my friends, but it is the truth. My son is the only male child of August Triano."

Rudy finally spoke. "How in the world….."

"What happened?" Morgan asked, appropriately astonished.

Angelique went on to describe a loving relationship between August and her. August gave her a cottage of her own and spent most of his nights with her and Antonio. She was so in love with August that their age difference didn't often cross her mind, but in February 1972 it became apparent in a hideously devastating manner. As August jostled with the toddler Antonio, he began sweating profusely. In mere moments he lay unconscious. August had suffered a massive stroke. He was taken by ambulance to St. Helena General Hospital where he remained unconscious until he died two weeks later. Angelique tried to visit him, but Rosa was his only living adult relative and she issued orders to prohibit visits from anyone who was not blood related.

Four days after August died, a limo slowly meandered up the dirt road towards Angelique's cottage. A dust cloud followed. It was the final curtain call on Angelique's happiness. When the car stopped in front of her door four rugged looking men got out. Jorge and Marguerite were sitting in the passenger compartment like the condemned awaiting execution. The four men escorted Angelique into the limo with only a diaper bag as luggage. Rosa had given Jorge $3,000 cash, stuffed him into the limo, and told him he was no longer needed at the August Triano Winery. He could go wherever he chose, but she informed him that his daughter Angelique and Antonio were being escorted to Mexico. One of the four men who came for her advised Angelique that if she tried to return to

America, she and her son would be terminated. Jorge and Marguerite stayed with Angelique and returned to Mexico with her.

Angelique stopped and waited for Morgan or Rudy's reaction. Wasn't it insane to accuse August Triano's daughter of such treachery? They didn't. They were just small town cops, but they had heard the rumors about Rosa Triano and her connection with the New York mob. Besides running the winery treachery was her business.

Angelique remained in Mexico for two years before she tried to get back into the States. She did not have a birth certificate. She worked for a while in a variety of resorts in Cancun. She saved her money and waited for her chance to get back to the U.S. It took her eight years before she had enough money and nerve to head back north. She paid a man three thousand American dollars to get her across the border. She and Antonio were crammed into the back of a box truck with twelve other Mexicans who were going north to find work. They crossed the border south of Sierra Vista, Arizona and walked into the city from there. Angelique found a public restroom where she cleaned up thoroughly and dressed Antonio in his Sunday best. They checked into a local hotel as Angelique Sanchez and Jose Garcia.

"My son has been Jose Garcia since that day. If there is no Antonio Triano, there is no danger of him being terminated, as they say."

Everybody has an interesting life, but they need a big event. Even the most boring lawyer will have at least one big case where he's elevated in stature. Any police officer who's been around for a while will get that one big pinch that gives him a little notoriety. That's to be expected in a world where crime creates villains and heroes. Angelique was a mother and woman who just wanted to have a life. Still her entire existence was a big event. Morgan was enthralled by her story. He wasn't any closer to finding her son, but everything had changed. Morgan didn't think a strong loving woman like Angelique would raise a son who would steal and lie. Rudy was just as much converted. He leaned forward in anticipation waiting for her tale to continue.

"I have a good job. I manage the Quality Inn on A1-A. It's a ten-minute drive from here when the traffic is clear. I don't have a driver's license so I'm very careful. I have enough money saved to buy a little house in the Hispanic neighborhood near Plankton Boulevard. I'm happy here with my people, but I want a yard and flowers."

Illegal immigrants don't have bank accounts or credit cards, let alone IRAs, investments in stocks or 401K plans. They stick their money into their mattresses or into a coffee can or hide it in their ceiling tiles. They pay their bills in cash and buy money orders to send to relatives back home. If they're lucky enough, their families will deposit money in a local bank and transfer some of it to an American affiliate where it can be withdrawn. Their money never works for them and it never grows. If Angelique had enough money saved to buy a house, she had shown extraordinary discipline.

As Angelique contemplated the next portion of her story, Morgan's mind wandered. He didn't like being a bounty hunter. He would have preferred something more worthy of his twenty five years in law enforcement. There was a fascinating case presenting itself to him right at that moment. Wouldn't it be fantastic to help a deserving woman establish her citizenship and give her son back his identity? Jose was probably entitled to a portion of the August Triano fortune. Now that was a case worth pursuing.

Angelique continued in a more careful tone. "My son is wanted for something he didn't do. I've seen the wanted posters. We all have," she said, turning her hand toward the others who were quietly watching. "Most people here have never seen $20,000, but there isn't one among them who would collect a reward for Jose's arrest."

A low murmuring followed her remarks. "Jose esta innocent man," one of them said mixing his Spanish and English Angelique gave him an approving nod.

The first part of the story was complete. Angelique's life became a mundane caricature of Mexican life in the shadows. She made her way to south Florida where she cooked, cleaned and worked as a receptionist at several different hotels. Diligence enabled her to find her way into management. The position she held at the Quality Inn paid very well, and by the grace of God she had never been questioned by Immigration nor a Social Security agent. During that time Jose attended and graduated high school with honors. He worked while he was in school and learned several skills in the construction industry. Although he was a certified, electrician, plumber and skilled drywaller, he was still on the peripheral of American life. Jose was a good son. He was never in trouble and never associated with gangs or got involved with drugs or alcohol. Even now when he was 39 years old to find his name on a wanted poster was devastating to Angelique.

Angelique explained that Jose went to Memphis with a construction crew to build a warehouse for Fed Ex, but before the job was complete the local union went on strike leaving Jose's crew with the option of crossing picket lines or sitting it out. Jose chose to sit it out. He thought the strike would be over quickly so he answered an ad for gardener and landscaper at the Harmon Edison estate. He went for an interview and was hired on the spot. He took his orders from a large black man who was supposed to be the security guard, but he seemed to have many other activities Jose suspected had nothing to do with his duties. Jose noticed right from the beginning that nothing seemed normal behind those gates. Middle Easterners in Arabian garb arrived in limos in the middle of the night for brief visits. The activity surrounding their arrivals often included shuffling young women or moreover girls from one vehicle to another. He was suspicious that it was some kind of illegal escort service, but the fact that Edison was rich beyond imagination left Jose doubting that Edison needed to peddle whores.

There was a young woman who lived with Edison. Her name was Sonya Isles. Jose became acquainted with her, enamored in fact, and through her he learned the truth behind the clandestine stirrings. Harmon Edison was selling the young woman and girls he rescued from the streets to Saudi Arabian royalty and desert Sheiks. Girls who were no more than ten years old were being given into sexual servitude to vile and wicked monsters who treated women like animals. The female children were lusted after, but in reality they were less respected than cattle to their captors. Sonya Isles knew the sordid details. She had once been a target herself, but Edison latched onto her for some inexplicable reason and excluded her from becoming chattel for those red-eyed, Middle Eastern devils.

Sonya had a daughter. She was pregnant when Edison found her. Edison didn't have the same affection for the child as he had for Sonya, but she was worth at least $250,000 to him. She was a beautiful child with eyes deeper than any ocean. She was only five years old, but Arab demons drooled at the prospect of having her in their beds. On all the earth these were the most demonic and morally corrupt beings God ever sent down the pike. Sonya knew that Edison would sell her baby to the highest bidder. The thought was so painful it nearly drove her insane. In desperation she confided in Jose. There was danger in merely knowing about Edison, and even more peril in what Jose did as a result. He smuggled the child off the property in a trash container and fled.

"My son is in grave danger. I'm telling you this because I know time is running out. You look like cops, and I'm hoping that God has sent you, not the Satan who trades in human suffering."

"How do we know any of this's true?" Rudy asked.

Angelique turned to one of the men who were waiting like obedient servants. "Get the child," she said.

In just a few moments the man was back. A five-year-old girl ran ahead of him and into

Angelique's arms. "This is Anna," she said.

In the dim glow of the firelight, her eyes glistened and the deep blue of heaven radiated from them. Morgan had seen those eyes before. They weren't then the eyes of a child, but the eyes of the young woman who sat on the staircase in Harmon Edison's home. There was no doubt in his mind; this child was her daughter.

"God, what are we gonna do now?" Morgan said almost under his breath.

Chapter Fourteen

Two old retired cops whose experience was in the ways of small town life, were now thrust into a different theatre where their mettle would be tested. This stage was bigger and the plot more complicated. They left Angelique and went back to the Sea Breeze Inn to reflect on what they had learned. Reporting back to Anderson was now a thing of the past. They would use the money they were given to conduct an investigation, but it wouldn't benefit Anderson or Edison. Five thousand bucks wasn't much money, but it would buffer the cost of doing business.

When Morgan and Rudy talked about their dilemma, they both acknowledged that they were in over their heads. Between them they had almost fifty years of assessing and judging difficult situations but they had never seen anything like this. Breaking up fights and settling family disputes was easy stuff. Solving an international slavery case involving multi-millionaires was way out of their league and they knew it. Protecting a wanted Mexican without a true identity from murderers and hit men might even get a little hairy. Now as they thought about their strategy, Morgan determined he would do as he had always done. He would just do the right thing. Finding ways to do it was a whole 'nother matter.

As they sat on the bed in Morgan's room contemplating their next move, Morgan suggested that they take their case to the FBI. Rudy quickly nixed the idea. "What if they find out about Angelique?"

"You're right. We don't want her deported."

"Besides that, she's a US Citizen, she just can't prove it. That sucks," Rudy said.

With that being said, Morgan cracked open the laptop and began searching the web for articles on Arab nations where American girls were employed for entertainment. There were two magazine reports on network TV including interviews with women who had spent time in Saudi Arabia. There were several articles in national magazines, but nothing specific about slave trade but the implication was strong. It was all about exploitation. Both television reports and magazine articles hinted that some participants had diplomatic problems when it was time to come home. There was never an investigation by the State Department. It was insane that a condition like this could exist without the US Government becoming involved, but plainly that was the case.

Rudy called back home to run Harmon Edison and Anderson's names through law enforcement files. There were numerous hits on both names, but without birthdates and Social Security numbers they were no closer to criminal histories than they had been before they started. There were two Harmon Edison's in Tennessee, and one Anderson Claypool, but their ages and physicals didn't match. Morgan had signed up with an investigative data gathering agency he had used for skip traces, so he ran their names through their files. They came up big on Harmon Edison, but his

127

acquisition of wealth had been a quick ascension. There were no records of property before sixteen years ago but cash transactions and property purchases were plentiful. He was extremely wealthy but the records didn't show how he acquired his millions." Morgan and Rudy knew, but proving it was another matter.

The only asset they found on Anderson Claypool was a 401K plan totaling 78,000.00. The contributing employer wasn't listed. They suspended their efforts at that point and settled in waiting for Angelique to contact them again. They wanted to talk to Jose to learn as much as they could about Harmon Edison and his operation. It would be several days before their wait was over.

It had been a week since Anderson had given Sonya the laptop and some hurried instructions. She was quick; her mind was a sponge, and she learned rapidly. She found that her shopping account had only a $1,000 balance, so she traced the deposit transactions back to a very substantial account maintained by Edison for her general use. She transferred $150,000 into that account. And with that she opened a separate account in her name only. She rented a post office box online and had her debit card sent to the post office box. Edison had kept her isolated from the world for six years, so her identity was as much a mystery to her as it would have been to anyone else. She knew that she could get her school records from the University which she ordered online, and a copy of her birth certificate from the State of Arkansas. Her airline tickets were purchased and would be waiting at the airport when she arrived. A photo ID was mandatory for boarding the plane, but she didn't have a driver's license. She found that she could obtain a State of Tennessee non-driver's photo ID, but she had to make the application in person at a local driver's license facility. That could be handled at any walk in location in the Memphis area. When that happened, she knew all strings would have to already have been cut.

In the middle of the night Sonya slipped out the patio door and into the vast back yard. She quickly crossed the lawn and scaled the wrought iron fence that spanned the cliff above Riverside Drive. There was nothing but a foot of ground between the fence and a deadly 150 foot fall. She hung onto the fence and edged her way across to the neighbor's property and ran for Tennessee Street. And freedom.

Anderson was watching from the guard house closed circuit. He switched the oscillating camera from manual back to automatic. He had held it just long enough for Sonya to sprint for freedom. She didn't know he was watching, or that he was aware of her departure. She didn't ask questions about his involvement. Anderson could only think that she believed he was a good-hearted southern black man who wanted to see a little bird fly. In the pit of his stomach he knew he was a contaminated soul, but it soothed him to think there was goodness left within him.

Chapter Fifteen

In Rockford, Illinois, a seemingly unrelated situation was about to start a chain of events that would bring together an unlikely entourage of people from very different walks of life. A young Arab was helping with hand signals to guide a semi into the bay of a loading dock at the Bostonian department store. His name was Ajith Aswami, but everybody at Bostonian knew him as Keith. He had been employed as a dock employee for the last three years while attending Rockford University as a full-time student, putting in 35 hours per week unloading trucks. He was a good employee. Unlike many of his fellow workers he always followed security procedures and the security director had tried to recruit him into the security department several times, but he had declined. He was happy working on the dock, and all his coworkers liked him. However, things were about to change. A few indiscretions in his life were about to catch up with him - things he hoped would never come to realization were upon him like an explosion.

The semi-trailer made contact with the unloading ramp as it stopped with a thud.

Ajith shouted, "Stop," an instant after it had already jarred the driver's eye teeth.

The driver jumped from the truck cab and

hurried inside. "Thanks, Keith. I nearly swallowed my tongue," he said lightheartedly.

"I said, stop." Keith laughed.

"Right after I backed through the backstop," the driver argued lightheartedly.

After a few other accusations about which of them was responsible for the rough landing, the driver started to open the rear trailer door.

"No! No!" Keith shouted. "There's a security seal on that door."

It was an aluminum strip with raised numbers that was clamped to the door lever, indicating there was a security manifest inside. Lifting the bolt would break the seal, a clear security violation.

"We have to have a security officer present to open this door and sign the manifest" Keith said.

"Let's just break it, nobody will notice," the driver said. He was in a hurry to get back on the road. Bostonian Department Stores were a chain out of Milwaukee and all deliveries came from the distribution center there. The driver had three other stores in the southern district waiting for deliveries. Most of the time security seals were ignored; especially if the drivers were in a hurry. It was different when Keith was dock attendant. If there was a security seal, then security would be present when it was unloaded. No exceptions.

Keith called for a security agent then waited. The driver had been in a great mood earlier, but now he was grumbling under his breath. Keith watched him with a faint smile.

"Patience, my friend, patience."

The driver smirked and grumbled quietly.

"The oxen is slow, but the earth is patient," Keith said, trying to restore the driver's earlier cheerfulness.

"Is that some ancient Arab proverb?"

"No, Chinese. An old Arab proverb sounds more like this, Yaleeyaleeyaleeeeyaleeyalee!," he shouted. Both he and the driver laughed.

Just then the security guard arrived at the dock, out of breath. He cut the security seal and quickly entered into the truck to find the required item marked for special security attention. "It's just a tote for the Fine Jewelry Department. Keith, stay with me until I get it to them, will you? Two people must be present when it's delivered. I'm in a hurry to get back to the break room. Something big just went down at the Army base a Fort Campbell. It's on TV right now. Geez,my brother is stationed there" he said.

After taking the security tote to the Fine Jewelry Department, Keith went with the guard. There were several people clustered around the TV studying CNN News. An Army major at Fort Campbell Kentucky had just killed twelve of his fellow soldiers in the induction center there. Early reports were that he was an Arab. The news reporters were careful not to imply that it was terrorism, but people in the break room were already speculating. The security guard had to push his way past several people who were glued to the TV. He waited for Keith to follow him, but Keith was standing as if paralyzed. His face was drawn and colorless. The security guard made his way back through and put his hand on Keith's arm.

"Keith, nobody will resent you for this. You didn't do it. Everybody here likes you. They know you're not sympathetic to terrorism," he said. Marty was looking for a sign as to what might be the reason for Keith's obvious despondency.

"I know, Marty, I know. Nobody will blame me." There was something else going on inside Keith's head that was much more disturbing than his concern for the views of his fellow workers. Marty slapped him on the back and headed off into the store.   Keith dropped the security tote onto the floor and started for the parking lot. He wasn't scheduled off work for another two hours, but he knew he had to go. His time had come He opened his cell phone and pushed the number 1.   After only a few seconds, someone answered.   Keith was getting into his Ford Expo preparing for his departure when he said, "It's time." This was the incident he had been ordered to watch for. It wasn't just another act of terrorism, but the event calling him to action. His orders were to report for duty when an attack happened in Fort Campbell, Kentucky. The event he hoped would never come.

All over the country young Arab men were dropping their tools, closing their desk drawers, and heading for their cars just as Ajith had done. They were in cells of six individuals to a unit, ten units in total. Ajith had been assigned a route driver because he knew how to drive a semi-truck. He didn't know the other individuals he would be working with. He knew only where he was to meet them. He knew where he was going, but he didn't know his assignment. He trusted that Allah would guide him and provide the answers. Deep down inside he believed this day would never come. He never expected that he would come to love this country, but somehow his mind had been altered and now he dreaded his destiny. Still Allah had called and it was his duty to respond.

He truly regretted getting involved in the Caliphate, but there it was looking him right in the face.

Marty was standing in the dock door watching Keith driving off the parking lot. He had memorized Ajith's vehicle description, serial number, and license number, but he was betting he wouldn't stay with the same car. He wasn't worried about where Ajiith was going. It wasn't his concern now this part of his job was over.

Marty walked into the dock office, opened the laptop computer and punched in a security code. In a matter of seconds he was online. A series of numbers appeared on the screen. He used the mouse to highlight numbers in different lines. The monitor went straight to a blank screen. He typed the sentence, "My man has taken leave." Once the message was encrypted and sent he picked up the computer and slammed it onto the floor. Now he needed to move on to another assignment.

Marty was part of that same secret organization Anderson Claypool belonged to and sworn to stop radical Islamic terrorism. The members were all people who had been affected directly by the World Trade Center murders. Marty had been assigned to monitor Ajith's activities; to know him; to befriend him. It was his job. He didn't expect to find him to be such an agreeable man. In spite of his efforts to the contrary, he had come to like him. Regret was his only emotion at that moment. Still he needed to move on, to vanish. He waited for only a few moments until a black Chevy sedan drove up to the loading dock and stopped. Marty hopped off the ramp and jumped into the passenger seat.

At that moment, Marty, the security guard, had ceased to exist.

Ajith's job had just begun. He had stepped onto the terrorism train, and that was a ride on dead end track.

At 5:00 p.m., the store manager stood at the dock overhead door. He had searched the entire facility for Marty and Keith, but both had disappeared. The overhead doors were open to anyone who might want to rob them blind, and the office laptop was in pieces on the floor. He placed his hands on his hips and stared out into the parking lot. "What the hell?" he mumbled.

Chapter Sixteen

High above Riverside Drive, Anderson Claypool keyed up his laptop and read the encrypted message. It wasn't necessary for him to use the decoding program. The new phase of the operation was going down. He made a quick entry, hit the send icon and waited. In just seconds his reply was confirmed. He picked up the computer and bounced it off the concrete floor. The event at Fort Campbell had changed everything. Things were beginning to move.

It was a short walk from the security center to the main house. The same woman who had greeted Morgan and Rudy let Anderson into the service entrance. "We need to vacate the premises, Thelma," he said.

"Yes, sir," she replied.

Protecting Sonya and recovering Anna weren't in Anderson's responsibilities, but it weighed heavy on his mind. It was the one thing he needed for a modicum of clemency.

Anderson's strides were quick and deliberate as he walked the long hallway towards Edison's study, his eyes focused on the double doors as though he could see beyond them and into the lush interior. If the fire behind his eyes could have transcended distance the doorway would have exploded in flames. He pushed through it and the heavy oak hit the door stop with a thud. Harmon Edison was startled and sprung to his feet. "What are you doing," he shouted. Anderson had only one responsibility to perform there at the Edison estate, and it was personal.

"Have you sent other hounds to find the child?" Anderson snarled.

"What's your problem, Claypool?" Edison demanded.

"Have you sent other hounds to find the child?" Anderson's roared.

"Of course. Those two idiots from Illinois wouldn't be able to find their butts with both hands! And besides that, what's it to you!"

Anderson didn't have a southern drawl and his slow languid movements had vacated the premises along with Thelma. There was thunder in his voice and fire in his eyes. "I sent them for that very reason, you fool! Now you've sealed your own fate!" Anderson bellowed.

Edison recoiled, walking away from Anderson to a location behind the couch. "Anderson, you're out of line. You need to leave. Now."

Anderson sprung over the couch like a huge graceful cat. Edison's expression turned from agitation to fear. He had no idea what was happening, but terror was rolling over him like a freight train.

"Anderson, please, it's not your concern. Would you please leave," he whimpered.

"How many?" Anderson demanded.

Edison started to walk away but Anderson's mighty paw came upon his shoulder, and with one hand Anderson spun him around.

"Several," Edison whimpered, barely having the strength to reply.

Anderson looked directly into Edison's eyes. Whatever substance there was left in him fled in a blink. Edison went limp and Anderson held him upright like a rag doll.

"Tell me!"

"They're already in Hollywood, Florida. Jose Garcia is at the Paradise Motel with his mother. I turned the operation over to Abib's assistant. Abib paid for the child. The whole thing is in his hands now."

Anderson released his grasp. He glared at Edison for a long moment, and then with power and grace Anderson's hand hacked through the air like an axe with a rush of wind behind it. He chopped Edison's throat with such force that his Adam's apple was shattered and his windpipe was detached. Edison clutched his neck with both hands and writhed in pain as he struggled for air. Anderson could have easily killed him instantly but he wanted to watch him squirm before he died.

Edison's eyes bulged, the muscles in his face twitched, and his eye sockets filled with blood. Just at the instant when the black curtain of death descended, Anderson leaned forward and whispered, "That's for Anna, Charley."

Harmon Edison, a/k/a Charley Heidbreider, lay dead on the floor of his study. Two men in black military garb entered the room and quickly slid his carcass into a body bag and carted him out the back door. A black Chevy sedan drove up the driveway. Thelma got into the back seat. The truck lid flew open and Edison was stuffed inside. The two men in black slipped into the car and drove away.

Anderson walked past the wrought iron gate and sauntered north on Tennessee St. It really wasn't his job to save the child, but deep inside; way down below the calloused surface, there existed that glimmer of human kindness that God bestows on all his children. Being around Sonya and her child had softened him ever so slightly and caused him to hope they could somehow be rescued.

He didn't really believe Morgan and Rudy would be able to save them, but he sensed they were good men. He knew that when he sent them after Jose Garcia they would eventually find him and learn the truth, at least part of it. Anderson was well learned in human behavior, and he was certain they would do the right thing. His worry was that they didn't have the skills to survive.

His theory was that Abib, the degenerate who had previously bought Anna from Edison, was involved in other more heinous endeavors of terrorism. He was certain he had provided financial support for other operations against America in the past. In part, he had provided monetary support for 9/11. After the 911 attack, Anderson had been deliberately placed with Edison in order to get next to Abib and his associates. If his duties lead him into Florida, then maybe he could save Anna and Sonya. He hoped Morgan and Rudy could stave off the onslaught until he found a way to assist them. Maybe he could send The Jesus impersonator to lend a helping hand.

In the meantime, he had the world to save.

*****

Back in Hollywood, Florida, Morgan and Rudy

were still waiting for Angelique to contact them to interview Jose. They had lost their focus regarding the entire case. Neither one of them had an idea what they would do next. They certainly weren't in it for a reward, and their contact with Anderson was permanently cut. They had reached that point where there wasn't anything in it for them.

They knew Anna was in good hands, and it was evident that Jose and Angelique would try to find a way to return her to Sonya. They had no way of knowing that Sonya was trying to find her way to Hollywood at that very moment, and that Edison had assumed room temperature.

After sleeping on the revelations heaped upon them at the Paradise Motel, Morgan and Rudy were beginning to think there was nothing they could do. They knew they couldn't go to the FBI without throwing Angelique under the bus, and they weren't equipped with the resources or knowledge to dismantle an international slavery ring without help. It would have astounded them to know that Anderson Claypool had already remedied that situation.

A more deadly condition was approaching them fast.

As sometimes happens when there are no answers, Morgan and Rudy responded by taking a walk. Having a beer seemed like a good idea. They left the Sea Breeze Inn and sauntered down the boardwalk to Sorrento's Italian Restaurant. The plastic wind curtains had been lifted and the beach side portion was open to the sea air. Small wooden tables were situated near the sidewalk and a breeze quietly rustled the palm leaves. A small retaining wall was all that separated sauntering tourists on the boardwalk from the beach. It was still early and the white sand was clean and smooth all the way to the water. A few college-aged girls were already lying on beach blankets and their boyfriends were up tossing a frisbee and drinking beer. The sky was blue all the way to eternity, and a smattering of puffy white clouds lingered on the horizon.

Morgan ordered two Bloody Mary's while Rudy pulled up a table. Rudy stared out into the ocean as if he were looking at it for the first time. He was like a man who had worked a crossword puzzle until he was completely stumped. He didn't want to go to the back of the book for the answers, so he pushed it aside. Maybe later he would have another shot at it.

Morgan joined him at the table with the spicy red drinks full of sausage and celery. "I thought we'd have breakfast instead of beer," he said.

"So, we're drinkin' our breakfast now, is that it?" Rudy said.

"Maybe it'll inspire us. Give us some ideas."

"I've got an idea, Morgan. Let's sell our houses, cash in our annuities and buy a condo down here together."

"People will say we're queer," Morgan said. He was a bleeding heart but he was a little behind on political correctness.

"I don't care what people say. I'm too old to attract women without having a gimmick. Maybe the laurels will attract a few gals who go for that kinda thing."

"Rudy, I'm married," Morgan said.

Rudy opened his mouth, but he caught himself

before he put his foot in it. He sipped on the Bloody Mary and turned to watch a newcomer on the beach feeding the sea gulls. "Even I know better than that," he said, holding his drink with three fingers and pointing at the fool causing the stir on the beach with the other one.

Morgan smiled. He had been guilty of feeding sea gulls before he learned it was taboo. As they watched the swarm of birds fighting for popcorn and screeching, they failed to notice a man hurrying down the boardwalk in their direction. He was dressed in a long white robe, wearing sandals. As he passed their location he pitched a tan canvass bag onto the paving stones and it skidded to a stop beneath their table.

"What's going on!" Rudy shouted.

"It's The Jesus again," Morgan said.

Morgan grabbed the bag and both he and Rudy gave chase. Jesus was younger and obviously more up to the task than either of them and the race was over in short order. Without benefit of a bomb expert on site, they took the bag back to the Sea Breeze for further examination. They found two 7-3122 Heckler machine guns, ammo clips and hundreds of rounds of 9 millimeter ammunition. There was a slick black object that appeared to be some kind of dense plastic block included. It was slick and completely void of letters or numbers. It looked like a paperweight.

Morgan shoved the guns under the bed (clearly a safe location for deadly weapons!) and stuffed the block into his pocket. They were still stumped about their next move. Their first walk garnered nothing but more mystery, so they decided to give it another try. After all, isn't the definition of insanity to try the same unsuccessful actions repeatedly while expecting different results? Morgan already thought Rudy was out of his mind so why not join him. With that, they took another walk.

The waves on the beach had receded and left a wide swath of hard sand with a knee-high shelf, a perfect place to sit and contemplate fate. Rudy stared out into the ocean watching the sailboats in the distance while a single engine plane dragged a banner across the sky advertising Leo's Crab Shack. Morgan sat with his hands between his knees studying the plastic block. They were there for an hour before their first clue became suddenly evident. A beeping sound started faintly, and then a bright green blinking light became visible deep inside the center of the block. Morgan and Rudy both sat up straight. A message scrolled across the box, "Two armed subjects 10 meters, 6 o'clock."

"It's 10:30," Rudy said.

Morgan turned and looked behind him. The message changed, "Two armed subjects 12 meters, 6:40."

"I think it means location, Rudy."

"Eighteen meters, nineteen meters, twenty meters, threat terminated."

"There's two Beach Patrol Officers going away from us, Rudy."

"What the hell!" Rudy whispered hoarsely.

"This thing is some kind of detection device," Morgan said.

"Then we can guess that it was tellin' us that there was two sand cops carryin' heat coming up behind us. That's nice, but do we need to know Beach Patrol is gainin' on us." Rudy laughed.

"Or anybody with a gun. That's some good technology, Rudy."

"You got that right. But who sent it?"

"Maybe Anderson?"

Chapter Seventeen

Sonya had seen airports on TV and depictions in movies, but this would be her first real life experience. She was afraid she wouldn't be able to negotiate her way through the process and find herself lost and without a plan. The cab driver gave her some helpful advice, which did little to calm her nerves. When he dropped her at the American Airlines terminal he assured her that there were many people inside who would be able to give her directions. She had studied the procedures online but she was still tentative. She found her way to a kiosk and followed the instructions for obtaining a printout of her boarding pass after which she isolated herself in a secluded location until she understood the information on it. The airport in Memphis is relatively small, but still big enough to be perplexing to someone who had never been in one before. She was anxious and frightened but she had no trouble finding her way to her gate. When they called for her boarding pass she was trembling. As her ticket was checked, the pilot was watching her. He was quick to notice her anxiety. But who wouldn't notice her? She was alarmingly beautiful looking like the proverbial deer caught in the headlights. When she walked past him he said, "Don't worry, honey, it's just a big bus with wings." She returned the smile, grateful that he had noticed her. She felt better.

The long enclosed boarding ramp was claustrophobic and the narrow aisle inside the plan did not help to put her at ease. She worried about where she would put her carry-on until she watched other passengers stuffing all sorts of luggage into the overhead storage spaces. Some bags went in easily and others were pushed and hammered until they were mashed into spaces much too small for them.

A few people were quietly settling in, while others were noisy and boisterous. The passengers were dressed in sweatpants, t-shirts, sports coats and slacks, suits and pricey trendy dresses. Some of them had expensive luggage, and others had canvass bags and plastic sacks. There were people from all social and economic levels heading for Fort Lauderdale. It wasn't anything like Sonya expected.

Sonya's trip was an odyssey. As the jet propelled along at 400 miles per hour Sonya analyzed everything through the eyes of a child. She marveled at how the ground resembled a giant quilt pieced together by fields and highways and further that she could actually see how the landscape was formed by rivers and streams. Now she could see that valleys were honed by rushing water, and the mountainsides were grooved by the rain making its way to the sea. She didn't know she would be able to see the earth's curvature as the sun inched away into the darkness. She was surprised and fascinated that the sky was darker and a deeper blue. The city lights appeared to be smoldering embers from distant fires. She began to feel a rumbling in the pit of her stomach which she soon came to recognize as an exhilaration of the once remote possibility of her freedom. Could she be on the cusp of that freedom? If so, all she needed now was to find her child to be complete.

Anderson Claypool stirred with the nagging bite of revenge. As the old saying goes, it's a dish best served cold. It just didn't apply in this instance. Anderson had portrayed the wag for Edison for so long that the fire inside was like molten lava percolating to the surface. Satisfaction ran through him white hot as he watched Edison convulse into death. He was certain Edison was in the grasp of Satin himself, and if there were a hellfire Edison was submerged into a pit of never-ending agony.

Anderson often felt he had essentially traded his soul for revenge. He only hoped that because his actions were helping to save innocent people, his punishment might be mitigated on judgment day. His hatred was as deep and wide as an ocean, but ironically he was able to compartmentalize it and make Edison and the degenerates who were trading in human flesh his immediate focus. If he could successfully right that, that may serve as the first layer to calm him.

It was his old wound that had consumed him and that was far from over.

Ten years ago Anderson was a computer programmer. Revenge and hatred were as foreign to him as anything could be. His life was as mundane as a morning cup of coffee. He worked on programs designed to block pop-ups as he meandered through uneventful days. He was married to his high school sweetheart. Their days were consumed with raising eleven-year-old twin girls. In college Anderson was once on the fast track to the NFL, but he blew out his knee which in turn ended his dreams of glory, In the end he found happiness with Angie and their girls. He loved his life out of the spotlight. They lived in Davenport, Iowa where life was uncomplicated. Angie taught Government at Lewis and Clark High School. For two years she raised money for a field trip for her students to visit Washington D.C. and New York City. Once her monetary goals were met, she took twelve students and the twins and set out on the journey of a lifetime. They saw the White House, the Capitol, and many monuments in Washington, D.C. They had only one stop to make in New York City before their return trip home - the World Trade Center. The date was September 11, 2001. It was the last thing she would ever do.

That was the day Anderson's life and his mind turned into a receptacle for hatred and revenge. As the reality of the situation set in, he was washed in unbearable pain and rage. He was left without the strength to stand, or sit, or even to lie down. As the twin towers crumbled to the ground, the image was emblazoned forever into his memory. Angie and his girls had died in a fiery inferno. It was a terrorist act perpetrated by people who stupidly believed our nation was too godless to exist. The whole idea was despicable and without intelligent rationale. Anderson was left a hollowed-out shell. As the weeks and months drug on, the emptiness was replaced by a raging desire to even the score.

Now in November 2010, after departing Memphis, he was on I-24 heading south to an unknown destination. He had already killed six men this week and he was embarking on a plot to kill another. A man he hardly knew was with him. Raja Kahn was in the passenger seat quietly contemplating his life in retrospect.

Raja was born at the St. Francis Hospital, Peoria, Illinois. He was Catholic. His Muslim parents immigrated to the U.S. after the Shaw of Iran was toppled in 1979. After many years in the States they converted to Christianity.

Raja was baptized at the St. Mary's and Joseph Catholic Church on November 12th, 1982. Raja was raised in the Best Western Inn at Prospect and Main where his dad was the live-in manager. He graduated from Manuel High School. Raja had never seen a Koran and had never attended a mosque in his life. After 9/11 he was subjected to a little prejudice but he understood and dealt with it. Nobody had to explain the hatred people felt for the radical Muslims who murdered over 3,000 of our innocent citizens. Raja's parents were standing at the foot of the World Trade Center when it crumbled to the ground. They were buried in 18 feet of debris and ash. Raja understood the hatred firsthand.

The sunshine intermittently cast golden streaks across the blue mountaintops and hung like an amber curtain on the misty hillsides as the road meandered lower into the Tennessee River Valley. Raja had never been in Tennessee before today. As they cruised down the mountainside overlooking NickaJack Lake, he was captivated by the majesty and beauty of it all. They were about an hour out of Chattanooga, en route to complete an action he would have scoffed at a few years ago. There was an awesome responsibility awaiting him. He dreaded the task but he knew it was his duty and he was ready. The grandeur of the mountains diverted his thinking away from the pending mission. It was a welcomed distraction.

Ajith Asammi was in a car ahead of Anderson and Raja, a dock worker known as Keith just a few days ago was now known as the "target" to Anderson Claypool. Keith was so submerged in thought that he hadn't noticed the car following him. He was wrestling with his conscience over what he was going to do. He dreaded that this day had come. When he joined the movement he never believed it would be more than a political resistance to American occupation of the Holy Land and the birth of an Islamic State. Sure, he was told that there would be violence but he believed he would only be philosophically engaged. He didn't want to actually be in on the fight. Still he thought Allah was guiding him and in control of his destiny. It didn't matter that he might be more American than he was Arab, he still had to be a good Muslim soldier. Still he would rather be working on the loading dock at Bostonian Department stores going about the business of making a living.

It would be great if it was known what follows death, and there really is a God in Heaven? If God exists is he the God of all people, and does he have a plan for us? Are there many gods? Do they live for eternity, or do they die? Is our God dead?

There are people in all religions who say they know. Christian preachers on Sunday morning TV say they know. They say God lives in every human being, and in every tree and plant. They see his works all around them. They say heaven awaits a faithful believer and hell is eminent for unrepentant sinners.

Jesus is the Son of God and he is the only way, the truth and the light.

Muslims, Jews, and Buddhists have their beliefs. They're just as adamant about it as Christians. Muslims believe their god has commanded them to rid the world of Christians, Jews, and all non-believers. Al-Qaeda and other radical Islamic elements have put legs on their beliefs and wheels on their prayers. Bowing to the east at sundown and praising Allah didn't cut it anymore. Now Allah required blood.

Death to the infidels!

Nobody has ever crossed the ravine between life and death and returned to enlighten the world. What exists on the other side is a matter of faith. Anderson Claypool wasn't concerned about faith or scriptures. It didn't make a damned bit of difference to him if terrorists were Muslims, Christians, Buddhists, or Satin worshipers. If they were involved in terrorism, he was going to help them cross the divide. God could sort them out in the afterlife.

Anderson perked up as the maroon Honda with Illinois plates turned off the interstate. Raja studied Anderson's face for a reaction but his expression didn't change. His demeanor remained calm but the intensity in his eyes betrayed him.

"We have to make this quick, so be ready to respond immediately to everything I say." Anderson said.

Raja tried to stay on an even keel but his body language screamed hysteria. He had wanted this for ten years, but now that it was here his stomach was churning. He knew when the rubber hit the road Raja would react properly. He had no other choice.

"Have you gotten rid of all your identification cards or other things showing who you are?" For the moment Raja Conn would temporarily cease to exist.

"Yes."

"Do you have cash?"

"Yes."

"Then just do as I say and everything will be fine."

"I will."

The Honda drove onto a Shell station service drive. It was dusk and the roadway was damp from the heavy humid air. The surrounding light waned into a dreary haze. The gas station was across the street from the return ramp onto I-24. There was only one customer there. One potential witness didn't concern Anderson.

Ajith Aswami didn't see Anderson proceed to the end of the blacktop service lane. He finished filling his tank and paid the attendant with cash. As he entered onto the roadway to return to the interstate Anderson slowly passed in front of him. Ajith followed as they approached the stop sign. Anderson reached inside his coat and fetched a 22 magnum revolver. He eyeballed Ajith in his rearview mirror. He screwed the silencer into the gun barrel with a skilled hand. Raja watched and waited.

Anderson increased his speed. Ajith followed suit. In a split second Anderson slammed his brake pedal. Ajith was quick to respond but it was too late; his front bumper banged into Anderson's car.

Before Ajith could take a breath, Anderson was out of his car briskly heading towards his driver's door. Anderson had his cell phone to his ear. There was a red hand towel stuffed in his front pocket.

Ajith was frustrated. He didn't need this. He wasn't concerned about his car but he didn't want police involvement. By the way he disappeared from Rockford, he was concerned that there may have been a missing person's report filed on him. There wasn't anything illegal about disappearing, but he didn't want to answer questions.

"I'm sorry," Anderson said. "I dropped a cigarette in my lap and I panicked. It's totally my fault."

Ajith saw the small dent in Anderson's bumper. Although the accident was clearly Andersons fault Ajith's first thought was to flee, but his better judgment took over. That was the one sure-fired way to get the police department involved. His next thought was to offer money.

"It doesn't look serious, maybe we can settle this right here," Ajith said.

"Well, I was calling 911, but they have me on hold," Anderson lied.

"Maybe we can talk," Ajith said.

Anderson agreed. Maybe they could talk. After a few moments they decided to pull over into the mall parking lot across from the exit ramp. Anderson led the way. As they stopped in a secluded part of the parking lot Anderson hit the trunk release button. Ajith stopped behind him. Anderson got out of his car without hurrying. He was as calm as a man going to his mailbox. Ajith was unconcerned as he watched him coming. He was relieved they were settling this without filing an accident report. Anderson reached down and jerked the car door open. He placed the .22 magnum behind Ajith's left ear and the red towel on the back of his neck. The sound was no louder than a bottle of wine being popped. Ajith's eyes bulged, blood and purple matter gushed out of his head and onto the towel. Anderson applied pressure until the blood stopped oozing. He reached into Ajith's coat pocket and retrieved his wallet. He signaled for Raja to come. Raja was wild-eyed and breathing heavily. In one swift movement Anderson pulled Ajith's dead body from behind the stirring wheel and stuffed him into the trunk of his car. He closed the trunk lid. His face didn't reveal a trace of emotion as he stood silently examining Ajith's wallet and identification. He closed the flap and handed it to Raja.

"Your name is Ajith Aswami. Make sure you study the information on his driver's license and memorize his Social Security number. Never answer to Raja until this mission is over. Take his car and follow the itinerary," Anderson handed Raja a GPS the size of a credit card. "Put it in your wallet."

"I thought his name was Keith," Raja said quietly. His eyes fixed on the identification card.

"He was a terrorist, Raja."

"I know."

"Are you alright?"

"Yes."

"Then go."

Raja got into Ajith's Honda, and Anderson returned to his car. They left the parking lot and hit the return ramp to I-24 south.

Chapter Eighteen

Back in Hollywood, Florida, Morgan sat on his bed staring blankly at the black plastic block as his mind wandered. He missed Molly. He stopped mourning her while he and Rudy were involved in what he thought was a valid pursuit of a wanted criminal, but now that he knew Jose Garcia was actually one of the good guys he was beginning to think about his previous life. He was like a man who needed to scratch an amputated foot long after it was gone. He wanted to reach back and grab onto his memories. Morgan considered this mission as no more than a distraction, but it was a distraction he sorely needed. He was completely smacked down by losing Molly and grief had consumed him, but he was still alive; still breathing. It was true that he had gone to bed every night for the last three years hoping that he would drift into eternal peace, but every morning he opened his eyes, put on his pants and headed off into another day.

Morgan knew something about himself that even Rudy didn't know. There was something deep inside that would always hang on and never say die. As the old saying goes, when there is nothing left to hang onto except the will to hold on - then hold on. Morgan had passed that point a long time ago. Until now there wasn't anything left but still he held on.

155

Now Rudy was in there prodding him to "fill 'er up."
He was moving again. At first it was mechanical, just
going through the motions, but now there was a
glimmer of hope. He could almost feel himself in there
somewhere fighting to be the old Morgan Cooper. This
distraction had become effective enough to feed the
phantom inside scratching its way to the surface. It felt
good, but guilt wouldn't die without a fight. Morgan
wanted to cling to his misery because he believed it
would keep Molly's memory alive. It made him feel
guilty to separate himself from the agony in any
measure. He didn't really have a choice about longing
for his past life. He knew he would always be looking
back, but it was time now to move on.

Sonya Isles was leaving the airport in Fort
Lauderdale. Her introduction to Florida was the warm
air on her face and the swaying palm trees in the
parking lot. She waited for the cab as she sat on her
suitcase watching the low crisp clouds racing across the
sky. The contrast between Memphis and Fort
Lauderdale was intriguing. In the Mid-South the leaves
were usually gone by November, and the damp air was
often chilling. The buildings and homes in Memphis
were brick, substantial but predictable. The city was
being hit hard by the recession, making it appear grim
and desolate. Here in Fort Lauderdale the architecture
was diverse and the buildings were bright coastal
colors. Sonya was fascinated by the differences
between them. To say that it was a whole new world
would seem naive, but in reality she was as a newborn
colt let to run unfettered in an open meadow. She was
anxious to see Anna but having the sun on her face and
the breeze in her hair was sweet liberty, not just in her

mind, but tangible. For the first time in her life, she felt completely unchained.

When the cab arrived she asked to be taken to the Paradise Motel. The driver looked troubled as if he wanted to say something, but he remained mum. He loaded her bags into the cab and took her to her destination.

Chapter Nineteen

As fate would have it, Pedro and Maria were working their way back into Morgan and Rudy's lives. The scenario was so unlikely that only divine influences could have evoked it. They were nearly broke and should have been headed back to Mexico, but they worried about getting across the border without a passport. Neither Pedro nor Maria had a clue about such matters and merely scratching their heads had not produced an answer. If they needed a passport to get into the United States, wouldn't they need one to get into Mexico? At that moment they were sitting on a sidewalk on A-1A considering their dilemma. Maybe it was providence when an Arab man came to them and offered them a job. He was the owner of the newly constructed Majestic Hotel, a 12-story hotel just off the beach 500 yards north of the amphitheater. The construction workers had vacated the area. It was ready for the grand opening save for the landscaping. They accepted the offer without discussing wages or working conditions. The hotel owner assumed they were competent with flowers, shrubs and paving bricks. After all, they were Mexicans. Pedro and Maria were practiced at planting and harvesting cotton and they could pick the hell out of a peach tree, but landscaping was alien to them. It wasn't the perfect marriage of employer and employee, but the owner wanted someone who wouldn't ask questions. He wanted someone who would be satisfied working in shadows.

They were given a room in the basement next to the water treatment system, and boiler room. It wasn't a concrete dungeon like some of their former residences but it wasn't anything like the guest rooms in the hotel above them either. The room was carpeted with a queen-sized bed and a small bathroom with a shower. They were as happy as fat orchard hogs even knowing it was a temporary gig, and when it was over they would be back on the street. As for the time being, they would plant shrubbery and build retaining walls and keep their heads down.

At times the premises were as empty and hollow as the Overlook Hotel in "The Shining", but there were other times when young Arab men were moving about quietly, nervously watching the hallways and doors. Being illegal aliens themselves it was easy for Pedro and Maria to recognize the quick glances and frequent looks over the shoulder as activity common to someone who was up to no good. In their efforts to be nonchalant, they were as obvious as a horsefly in the milk jug. Pedro and Maria were much more artful at hiding in plain sight. After their first few days they were totally invisible.

The 12th floor of the hotel housed only one immense apartment. It was extravagant to the point of being gaudy. The hotel was closed to the public but there was an older man who dressed in Middle Eastern garb staying on the 12th floor. He had an entourage of several men and two teenage girls. Pedro and Maria had heard him called Abib. He was like a little king traipsing around in all his glory.

Chapter Twenty

Away from Fort Lauderdale in Fisher, Indiana, a quiet little community 68 miles south of Indianapolis, Lafayette High School was gearing up for their basketball season opener. It was a non-conference game with their archrival, Ada, Indiana. The game didn't have any significance to Tomahawk Valley conference standings, but it was often the biggest game of the year. There were only 3800 residents in Fisher but Lafayette was a community school with 1200 students. David takes on Goliath.

Basketball wasn't just an extracurricular activity in Fisher. It was a religion. Grown men and woman showed up at the gymnasium on Friday nights dressed in feathers and beads, and little children were done up in war paint. They were the Choctaws and they were fully prepared for the invading Ada Bulldogs. To say they were ridiculous wouldn't touch it. When it came to basketball all reason was put asunder. The truth was that there was never a Choctaw tribe anywhere near Indiana. They were native to Florida, Mississippi and Alabama. But as far as the residents of Fisher were concerned, Indiana was Choctaw central.

Before every home game the restaurants, bars

and businesses bustled with farmers, plumbers, lawyers and bankers, all talking basketball. On nights when the Choctaws played out of town, the highways and streets were flooded with traffic heading out to invade someone else's territory. The police department uniforms were Choctaw Indian colors, and the community library flew the Choctaw flag on game day. This was the first game of the season and the most important day of the year. The gym would be shaking like a hot stove, and Fisher fanatics would soon be stuffed together in the gymnasium like chickens in a hen house.

Anderson Claypool was leaving the airport in Indianapolis. He was following a yellow eight-passenger Dodge van. He had been in Indianapolis for several hours waiting for the van to leave the parking deck. Earlier in the day he had broken into it and thoroughly dusted the interior with IRDC-2 fluorescing powder. It was invisible to the naked eye but when exposed to a black light or an infrared night vision lens it would shine like a new dime. When he finished, he closed the van and relocked it. Anderson was a busy man.

The van was later occupied by Ahmed Sethi and seven other young Middle Eastern men. They were a cell out of South Bend, Indiana. Anderson called them Patels because nearly every Arab he knew shared the name. It was a bit insensitive but he didn't care. Killing them was a little insensitive too, but that didn't bother him either.

The van left the airport and headed south on Route 97, en route to Fisher. It would take about an hour and forty five minutes. If they stayed within the speed limits they would arrive right on time. Inside the van the men acquainted themselves with the AN94 Russian assault rifles and the U.S made M16's. They moved around in the van loading their pockets with extra clips and ammo and fitting themselves into bulletproof vests. They knew they were going down in a ball of fire but they wanted to stay alive until the end. At the same time they unknowingly wallowed in the IRDC-2 fluorescing powder.

The sun dipped below the tree line as the van headed into the rest area. With Prayer Pads in hand all eight men filed out of the van and took a position on the east side of the welcome center. They took off their shoes, faced Mecca and bowed to pray. Anderson stopped behind a blue Chevy with New York license plates. Two brothers, Sal and Anthony Paoletti, got out of the Chevy and got into Anderson's car, leaving their car behind. It wasn't just a chance meeting, It was prearranged. They were just lucky the van had stopped at that location..

"It's good to see you again," Anderson said.

They both shook Anderson's hand. They were glad to see him too. It had taken them all day to make the drive and they were tired but not so much that they weren't ready for their task. The two brothers were owners of The Big Apple Deli in New York City. Their father, Gustav Paoletti, opened the store in 1959 and the brothers worked side by side with him to make the deli successful. Neither of them could remember when they were put into service because they were introduced to the place while they were still on the teat. In 2001 both brothers were in their forties and just a bit pudgy from sampling their own deli goods. Things had changed over the last ten years. Now they were as fit as Olympic athletes.

On September 11th, 2001, Sal, Anthony, and Gustav watched as the World Trade Center smoldered. The smoke and ash was heavy outside but people still gathered on the sidewalks to watch in disbelief. Gustav left the shop against the urging of Sal and Anthony to go to his cousin Vito's restaurant 3 blocks away to check on Vito and his family. Before he reached Vito's restaurant the first of the twin towers came down. The sky turned black, the earth shook and downtown New York turned into hell on earth. Sal and Anthony covered their faces with wet towels and searched for Gustav. When they found him he had already suffocated. Before he died, his hide was peeled away from the bone by the heat and ash. Being caught on the street was like being hit with a blast from an atomic bomb.

Sal and Anthony were exhausted but they were up to the task ahead of them. Time, nor distance, nor fatigue would keep them from providence. They owed it to their father.

The sunshine diminished behind the hills as the eight Middle Eastern men piled back into the van. They were off again on their anointed journey. Everyone of them knew they were going to die but believed they were being guided by Allah. America was the Great Satan; the enemy of mankind. They all knew they would be remembered as a martyr in the afterlife. Collectively, they knew they were moving closer to it by the moment. All were prepared to die to defeat the Great Satan. This would be their moment in the sun and all the earth would know that Allah is great and evil would perish. They were true believers.

Anderson Claypool didn't agree. He thought their great moment in the sun would pass like an eclipse. He thought it would come and go without the world taking notice. As darkness gradually engulfed the landscape, the trees and hills became shadows. Anderson raised the night vision scope and scrutinized the eight glowing figures inside the van as he followed them down the roadway. He handed the scope to Sal and then to Anthony giving them each a peek. The bodies shined inside the van like fireflies in a garden on a hot July night.

The gymnasium at Lafayette High School was crammed. The body heat had elevated the temperature to a boiling point. It was a pressure cooker rumbling a loose lid. There were war whoops and Indian dances in every space big enough to wiggle.

The yellow van arrived and maneuvered around the high school parking lot until a parking space was found in a dark secluded location. It was at least a football field from the gym but Ahmed wasn't concerned about the distance. None of them would be coming back. They would use the assault weapons to kill as many fans as they could and then they would ignite the plastic explosives wrapped around their waists to bring down the house. The slaughter before the explosion would be just for show. He knew the local TV station had a closed circuit signal back to the studio and the entire rampage would be taped. Every savage detail would be seen worldwide once the networks got ahold of it.

Anderson Claypool didn't think so. He thought the evening would end with a few fistfights in the stands, and then the whole event would be regurgitated back at the local taverns like they were after every other game.

Anderson, Sal, and Anthony strapped on the Maxraptor 3x medium range sniper rifles with night vision scopes and silencers. They were loaded with armor piercing ammunition. They scurried up the steel ladder to the rooftop of the gymnasium and took a position along the wall. They fixed the guns to tripods and waited. Their wait was short. Eight fluorescent figures exited the van like a string of Christmas lights and began fanning out across the parking lot. Anderson took aim and a quiet burst from the Maxraptor left one shimmering mass flattened on the ground. Sal and Anthony followed suit. One by one the fluorescent glowing orbs became lifeless bodies on the ground. There was one light left moving as Anderson took aim.

"I guess this one will cause the big boom," Sal said as he watched through his scope waiting for Anderson to take the shot.

"I don't think so that stuff he's carrying is plumber's putty," Anderson said as he closed one eye and centered the sight. He had replaced the explosives with something pretty benign. In the next instant Allah opened his arms and another martyred soul was welcomed into the afterlife.

"They sho is some good Patels down dare on da ground," he said, mimicking his former southern black drawl. Sal and Anthony laughed.

A black van circled the parking lot silently and picked up the corpses. Anderson watched as he dangled his legs from the rooftop. At one location near a shimmering body the flash from a gun blast lit up the night. The sound was no louder than a fizzling firecracker.

"I guess that one was still moving," Anderson said.

When the bodies were gathered and the black van was gone, Anderson flipped a set of keys to Sal. "Those are to the yellow van. Take it to the rest area where you left your car. It will take the police a few days to figure out that it's been abandoned. Ahmed won't mind."

They shook hands and vowed they would meet again. Sal and Anthony were exempt from the no names rule. They had been with Anderson from the beginning.

Chapter Twenty One

Back in Hollywood, Morgan had enough time to examine the plastic block. He found there was actually a touch control enabling the device to be turned off and on. The weapon detection component couldn't be disabled, but he found that once the device was activated he had access to a global positioning service, the internet, and a tracking systems program too. He suspected there were numerous uses and applications included that he wasn't savvy enough to comprehend. Morgan was totally technologically challenged but he knew this thing wasn't on the market. It probably worked by sending out radio waves, or digital impulses to detect metal shapes like weapons and then returned a signal back to the block.

The moon had taken reign over the evening sky as Rudy returned from meandering up and down the beach. He wasn't concerned with Morgan's little magic plastic block. He was more impressed with how many French-speaking Canadians there were on the beach. He generally referred to them as Knucks in an affectionate sort of way. Rudy was amused by the many languages being spoken that he didn't understand. There were others who weren't nearly as impressed. "Are we still in America?" was a frequent rhetorical question from visitor who hadn't been there

167

before. The truth was that it had been like that since Rudy was a pup, and that was many moons ago. There were as many Russians, Eastern Europeans, and Hispanics running the restaurants and bars on the strip as there were Knucks on the beach.

Hollywood was a diverse and interesting place, and Rudy loved it. It was never in his plan to be on vacation but it seemed more like a holiday than an investigation. Morgan was more serious about the situation but that was only because he was a more serious person. In spite of himself, he was settling into that mindset too. He clearly wasn't interested in finding Jose Garcia. He turned out to be a first rate hero. He didn't think he could remedy the white girl abduction thing without going to the FBI and he had ruled that out. He was a little concerned about The Jesus scooting the automatic weapons under his seat. He might find himself in little hot water if the guns had been used in a killing or two before he started babysitting them.

In Fisher, Indiana, the Lafayette Choctaws polished off the Ada Bulldogs without a hitch. Al Qaeda's elaborate plan had ended without having bullet-ridden fanatics lying, smoldering in the charred remains of the gymnasium. The closed circuit telecast of the game was broadcast in every restaurant and bar in Fisher without a hint of violence. It had been a good day and a perfect start to the season. There were a few black eyes and bloody noses as usual, but there was no terror. The young Arab bodies disappeared into the night, and the wages for their sacrifice was an anonymous death. They went into the blankness of the abyss without their names being put to print. Praise Allah!

At that same time in a sleepy little town of 317 people, Hawthorne, Alabama, Al Qaeda operatives were pre-cooked to murder every man, woman and child who lived there, and to leave it in flames. Two sleeper cells out of Florida were set to invade in the middle of the night and snuff out every living being. But just as Lafayette High School had survived, so would Hawthorne, Alabama. There were others like Anderson Claypool lurking in the trees, lying in wait. When Al Qaeda came they were eradicated quickly and silently. Their bodies were gathered and hauled away like so much clutter.

On a ski slope in Nederland, Colorado, where the plan was for the sun to rise on snow-covered hillsides, saturated with blood and littered with bodies. Helicopters would hover over the slopes while astounded news reporters commented on the devastation. The newscast would go out all over the world and fear would ring throughout the land. That was the way terrorism was designed to work. But there was a hitch. It never happened. Men, young and old alike, came from among the trees and out of mounds of snow and silent flashes from automatic weapons cut them down and sent their souls tumbling into the hereafter. Their bodies were collected like game taken in a hunting expedition and evacuated undetected into the night. That was the power of the 9/11 Survivor Group (SG).

American law enforcement agencies were never involved. They were consumed with the protection of airports, national tourist attractions and major cities. The FBI and Homeland Security knew Al Qaeda had changed gears, but they didn't know how.

169

They didn't know Al Qaeda was trying to concentrate their activities on smaller and more numerous targets. Both agencies were trying to claim credit for the absence of another colossal attack on the country like 9/11. The 9/11 SG didn't care about credit. They just wanted results. Anderson's group were stopping runaway trucks from plowing into Fourth of July gatherings and local concerts. They didn't want credit or recognition, just results.

In the whole of things, there was a monumental screw-up looming on the horizon. U.S Attorney General Eric Holder announced his intentions to try the World Trade Center mastermind in a criminal proceeding instead of a military tribunal. Although Congress and the President were eager to support his intentions in the beginning, they were balking at the idea once public outrage reached a fever pitch. President Obama was losing support from the left and right after terrorists began to slip through homeland defenses. The FBI should have known there had been many other attempts, but Anderson's 9/11 SG organization was so thorough in cleaning up after themselves there was no evidence left for scrutiny. Still, some agents knew about them. They may have known about the Fisher basketball game, Hawthorne, Alabama, and Nederland, Colorado, and left it to destiny. With all the technology accessible to the FBI and Homeland Security, to think they didn't suspect something was happening was as likely as missing a snake in your lunchbox. There were agents within both organizations who resented the Obama Administration and feared them as much as they feared Al Qaeda. After all, Obama refused to use the term "war on terror" or to acknowledge terrorist acts had occurred until it smacked him square in the face. There were many lawyers in the Justice Department who had defended prisoners at Guantanamo Bay, and now wanted to prosecute former CIA agents for their interrogation techniques. It left agents uneasy. It was likely that some of them were feeding inside information to Anderson's organization because they wanted the job done but were handcuffed in doing it themselves.

Anderson Claypool wasn't the leader of the organization. He was only a soldier on the front lines. He didn't know his superiors, and the company didn't have a name. And yet, the organization had a thousand members. The common thread holding them together was that they were all linked to 9/11. Some of them were survivors and others were relatives of victims. They operated in secret and they were well-funded. The government had awarded them billions and they were still doling out cash. In March 2010 seven hundred billion dollars was awarded to first responders who were damaged by the ash and smoke while they searched for survivors in the aftermath. The members were drafted into service by various methods. Anderson was approached after he repeatedly returned to Ground Zero to grieve. The woman who contacted him was Thelma. They became partners, and friends.

Members didn't know when or how they would be activated. The last event was prompted by the terrorist attack on the processing center at Fort Campbell. It was the latest thing that Anderson was called into action for, due only to the fact that the occasion was also a call for Al Qaeda. cells to motivate. It was uncommon for the organization to know in advance of a planned terrorist act and fail to prevent it. They were like a well-oiled machine. The Fort Campbell incident seemed like an Al Qaeda success, but Anderson knew there must have been a far grander plan than to shoot twelve soldiers. He knew his organization stopped some of it but that was the story that would never be told.

Anderson was like every other member in his organization. He knew very little in advance. Tonight was no different. Hollywood Beach was the next target. He had only a few hours to get to Fort Lauderdale and clean up the situation. Raja Kahn was a plant with the cell that was assigned to execute the attack. He knew the plan and he would be there to stop Al Qaeda in their tracks. He hoped he would be able to help Morgan and Rudy rescue Sonya and Anna as well.

Chapter Twenty Two

Raja Kahn, now known as Ajith Aswami, met three men in Jacksonville, Florida. Raja was nervous but Anderson Claypool had assured him that everything would be okay. By Anderson's account, the others had never met the real Ajith Aswami and knew nothing about him. It was likely they didn't know each other. Raja's fears were alleviated when he tried to produce Ajith's driver's license to his coconspirators and was promptly told to keep it in his pocket. The others didn't want to know his name or anything about him. The fact that he was there was proof enough that he was legitimate. There was a fourth man en route who would join them later.

All three men were college age of medium height and weight. The only thing noticeable common denominator was that they were Arab. All three were edgy and nervous. They were probably college students who had been recruited in Iran, Saudi Arabia or Iraq. It was just as likely they had come to the United States to join sleeper cells without a clear understanding of what was expected of them. Ajith Aswami clearly didn't want to blow himself up or kill a bunch of Americans. He had become habituated to American life and secretly hoped Al Qaeda had forgotten about him entirely. He loved his American life. He may have

173

pulled out of the plan when confronted with killing innocent people, but down in Chattanooga, Anderson Claypool popped the stopper on all that. These young men were probably in the same position. They may have been future doctors or scientists, given the chance. They might have changed the world. But now they were on a long train on a short track. Their religious leaders had beckoned them into service. If they refused, their futures were not only in jeopardy, their families were in danger too. It was all academic now because Raja had seen Anderson Claypool in action and he knew their numbers had already been punched.

The meeting place was in Langelier Park, an old minor league baseball field where Hammering Hank Aaron played Triple A ball. The place was long ago turned over to the Jacksonville Park District, and now only a few summer league games were played there. There was a brass plaque behind home plate with the legend of Hank Aaron facing the stands. Raja loved baseball. He was born a few blocks from O'Brien Field in Peoria, Illinois, the home of the Peoria Chiefs. They were a major league affiliate that bounced back and forth between the St. Louis Cardinals and the Chicago Cubs. Raja was a diehard Chiefs and Cubs fan, but Hank Aaron, an Atlanta Brave, was his all-time hero. He mused that they were conspiring to bring down the United States under the legend of Hank Aaron, an American icon.

It had taken Raja all night to get from Chattanooga to Jacksonville. Fog had settled on Langelier Park. The man they had been waiting for came out of the fog, materializing like a ghost. He had yellow eyes with dark circles beneath them. He was sinister and evil. Raja was immediately intimidated. The other three seemed just as uneasy.

"Praise Allah," he said.

"Praise Allah," the others said in unison.

He turned to Raja without exchanging pleasantries. "Dwelling upon thy weariness will drain thee of thy strength and rob thee of thy desires," he said quietly.

Raja froze in his tracks. He knew this was his code phrase. A lump immediately formed in his throat and his windpipe closed. His chest became tight as he tried to speak. Finally his voice cracked as the words were forced out. "I'm sorry sir, but shouldn't the proverb be: Dwell not upon thy weariness, thy strength shall be according to the measure of thy desire.

"God is good," the man said, smiling and placing his hand on Raja's shoulder. In that same instant a tinge of guilt inside Raja began to percolate. At some point in the near future he would be involved in killing these men. Suddenly he dreaded the task. The world was surely at war and these four men were terrorists. Their aim was to assassinate innocent people. Still, Raja felt like Judas leading Christ to crucifixion. He had to think of his parents to rekindle his determination. After all, he wasn't doing this for thirty pieces of silver. These were the same people who had murdered his mom and dad.

After a few moments Raja regained his prospective. His companions were there to execute mass homicide. They talked about it in cold terms as one might discuss the weather. The man with yellow eyes was clearly the man in charge. They all knew they were there to commit atrocities, but Yellow Eyes held the particulars.

Aside from killing people Raja's job would include driving a semi-truck. His qualifications were that he was employed by a logistics company in high school, parking semis on the terminal lot. At least those were Ajith Aswami's experiences. Now, it was his responsibility to negotiate an eighteen-wheeler from Boynton Beach to Hollywood. The trailer would be filled with young men armed to the teeth. His manifest was murder. He was assigned to drive to Banyan St. He would open the trailer door and allow the men to unload and the attack would begin.

Yellow Eyes' mission was that every person on the beach be gunned down. He especially wanted to kill the children, even the infants and toddlers. He wanted their bodies to be bullet-ridden and mangled. It would create a greater effect if there was mutilation. He hoped tourists would run into the ocean where they could be cut down in the water creating a blood wave onto the beach. The more gruesome the image, the better. Raja's guilt departed with the waves and his purpose was reinforced. He was dealing with people who were mentally and religiously unhinged, and they had to be stopped.

Yellow Eyes would ride in the semi cab with Raja. The others would follow, pulling a U-Haul full of chemicals. They would release a deadly gas into the air once the beach was saturated with blood and littered with the dead. They were all equipped with gas masks. If an escape was possible, they could retreat to the newly constructed Majestic Hotel. Help would be waiting for them there. If death was inevitable, they were expected to die with honor. Beyond that, Raja knew nothing. He hoped that Anderson would contact him with a plan.

The morning sun was obscured by a hazy sky on Hollywood Beach. Sea gulls were lined up on the beach looking out into the ocean as the waves pounded the beach. The sea went on forever as the gray mist hovered on the horizon and blended into the clouds. An overnight storm had put the water into an agitated state but the weatherman was calling for clear skies once the sun burned through.

Rudy bought beach chairs, and a Styrofoam cooler stocked with beer. He picked up two cups of coffee and dragged Morgan out onto the beach. They quietly watched the waves and sipped the hot coffee. A woman in her late forties passed them wearing a sheer cover-up. The beach was deserted but she chose a location close to them. She glanced at them as she smoothed her towel on the sand. They were surprised that she had chosen a place in such close proximity. Possibly she was a regular there and they had taken her spot. People were funny like that. They harbored ownership of that one little place in the sand like a treasure. She dubiously examined the sky. She didn't like the looks of it. Morgan and Rudy watched her curiously. She had a pretty face and thick dark shoulder length brown hair, likely color-treated. The sun shone visible through the thin layer of clouds, but it was like a sixty watt bulb behind a white sheet. The woman scanned the beach then looked at the sky again.

Without a hint of warning that Rudy had lost his mind, he shouted, "It's gonna be alright, honey. My friend here is a meteorologist and he says the sunshine is coming."

Morgan gulped the hot coffee; it was too hot. He spewed it into the air. The woman laughed. "Good, I'm ready for it," she said. She dropped the cover-up onto the ground and scooted onto the blanket. Rudy had a little glimmer in his eye.

Morgan picked the tender, loose skin off the roof of his mouth.

"Not bad," Rudy said, nodding towards the woman. Morgan took a quick look.

"You're not gonna be sittin' on the sidewalk bawling over that glance, are ya?" Rudy asked.

"Fuk on you, Rudy."

"No, I mean it. Take another look. She's hot, man."

"Rudy, with all the trouble you've had with women, you should just give up," Morgan scoffed.

"Morgan, I like women. They just don't like me." With that said, Rudy went into a diatribe about his third wife. "She said she noticed me at George Bennett's wedding reception because I was so boisterously happy. After we were married, she would shush me all the time. She was attracted to me because I was loud but when were married she would shush me! I was fatter when we met than I was when she left, but she was always tryin' to get me on a diet. Sometimes I'd try to sneak a sandwich and she'd come into the room and look at me like she'd caught me molesting the babysitter."

Morgan smiled.

"Did ya ever get caught eat'n a sandwich and the bite you took wouldn't go down? Sometimes I felt like I was chew'n with my whole head! My ears would be moving up and down and the tendons in my neck would be bulging like they were gonna pop! It was hard, man! It's nerve racking when somebody's glaring at you while you're eat'n a sandwich. Sometimes I thought I should just eat in the closet."

Morgan laughed.

"We was married less than a year before she started glaring at me like she hated me." He stopped and looked out into the ocean for a long time. "Yeah, I like women, they just don't like me. I was the same man on the day she walked out as I was when she walked in. I didn't change, so I guess it was her mistake, not mine."

"I like women too," Morgan said. He reached into the cooler and retrieved a couple of beers.

As the sun broke through the clouds the beach was washed in bright light. The ocean was transformed from gray to blue and tourists swarmed the beach. Rudy sauntered over to his new love interest but she stubbornly coveted her privacy. In a few moments he was back.

Around noon both Morgan and Rudy's faces were glowing red. The six-pack Rudy bought was gone and the old wife tales were exhausted. Morgan suggested moving to Nick's to grab some lunch and spend the rest of the afternoon under the canopy.

Morgan ordered a BLT, and Rudy asked for a grouper sandwich.

"Did you know both of a groupers eyes are on the same side of its head, Morgan?" Rudy asked.

"Yes, I did."

As they waited for lunch, an older Hispanic woman, a forty-something Hispanic man, a beautiful young woman and a little tow-headed girl walked past them. The man was a little old for the young woman, but certainly within norms of romantic acceptability. They could have been a family out for an afternoon sashay.

Morgan watched them for a moment before he realized it was Angelique. The young woman was the girl he had seen on the stairwell at Harmon Edison's home. The child was Anna. Logic would dictate that the man was Jose Garcia.

"Look, Rudy," he pointed.

"By God," Rudy said.

Rudy was quick to go to the boardwalk to attract their attention. Angelique was first to see him. She conferred with the others momentarily, then they joined him. Morgan fetched chairs from an unoccupied table nearby to offer them a seat. They exchanged pleasantries as Angelique introduced Jose and Sonya. "They look good together, wouldn't you agree?" she asked.

Jose interrupted, "I'm a little too old for her, but I'd be dishonest if I didn't admit that she is beautiful."

Sonya studied him admiringly. Their age difference was glaring, but her eyes were conveying a different message.

The fact that they were there suggested that they were looking for Morgan and Rudy and had found them. Angelique knew they believed Jose was innocent by the way they reacted to her story. Now that Jose and Sonya were there together it should put the whole burglary thing to bed.

Morgan and Rudy weren't active duty police officers. They were retired and neither of them had jurisdiction in Tennessee; even before they were put out to pasture. It was highly unlikely they would be able to influence the case.

Angelique was an intelligent woman but she had spent her life avoiding law enforcement. She had no idea how things were supposed to work. She was surprised to learn that cleaning up the mess would require the Shelby County State's Attorney in Memphis to drop the charges and vacate the warrant. She was disappointed but Morgan assured her it could be done.

Rudy volunteered to call the Communications Center back in Willoughby Hills and talk to the Dispatch Sergeant to get an update on the case. He walked out onto the beach to make the call. He was gone for only a few minutes before he came back wearing a puzzled expression. "Harmon Edison has disappeared and the reward has been withdrawn. They can't find him, Morgan."

"Does that mean the charges have been dropped?" Angelique asked, her voice raised in anticipation.

"No, it means the case is still open, but since Edison is the complaining witness they will have to locate him before they bring the case to trial."

"What will happen if they can't find him?"

Morgan explained there were a lot of "ifs" involved. If Jose were arrested on the warrant he would be officially charged, regardless of the circumstances. Still, he could bond out and obtain counsel. Counsel would most likely make a Speedy Trial Motion. The State would be forced to bring him to trial within 120 days. If Harmon Edison couldn't be found, the Judge would be forced to throw out the case for lack of prosecution. If Edison showed up within the 120 days, the State would be rushed into the trial without time to prepare. Sonya, Morgan, and Rudy would all testify on his behalf and he would most likely be found innocent. Since the evidence was insufficient in the first place, it was a no brainer. The other possibility was Jose could stay in Florida. The States Attorney wouldn't be in no hurry to bring Jose into custody without a complaining witness so he would just let the Statute of Limitations run out on it. After three years he would be free and clear. If he wasn't arrested for something else in the meantime, it would all go away.

"Since we're dealing in "ifs," what if Jose gets stopped for a traffic violation?"

"It would activate the warrant."

"When his driver's license expires, will he be arrested if he goes to renew it?"

"Yes. They always run a 27 before they reissue a license. In fact, they probably already have a stop attached to it."

Jose was quiet while Angelique questioned Morgan.

Finally he spoke, "If that's the case, I'll have to go back. I'm not gonna live in the shadows."

Sonya reached over and squeezed his hand. Rudy was mum throughout the exchange. He saw the expression in Sonya's eyes. The age difference between them was less than Antonio's and Angelique's had been. Being an expert on love he decided to interject. "Does Jose know the story you told us about August Triano, Angelique?"

"He does, but I haven't yet told Sonya."

At that time she reiterated the account she

had given them at the motel. Jose watched her as if he were hearing it for the first time. Sonya was quietly contemplating every word. She often glanced admiringly at Jose. Their lives were so different but so much alike. Unique conditions beyond their control had shaped their lives. When Jose took Anna and fled, it changed everything. Now fate had brought them together and she saw it as their destiny.

Sunlight faded into evening, and Morgan and Rudy continued to enjoy their new found friendship. They didn't know how things would shake out but it was decided that Jose would return to Memphis and take his chances. Morgan and Rudy would go with him. Sonya would confront Harmon Edison and tell him that she was now on her own. She would have to go to the depths of hell, however, to do it. due to Anderson Claypool's good graces.

The preliminaries had been set., but in the meantime, they would enjoy Hollywood Beach. It was a good place for a vacation. Their planning was all arbitrary, due to what was happening at that very moment that would put a damper on their fun.

Something significant would alter fate forever.

They didn't know at that moment they were being watched by Abib's men. They had been shadowing them all day. Abib knew Harmon Edison was missing, but it didn't matter. He had purchased the blue-eyed girl, and he was going to have her. After seeing Sonya, he decided that he was taking her, too.

Most Americans were ignorant about Al Qaeda, the Muslim religion and the reasons for the war in Iraq and Afghanistan. They didn't know why Al Qaeda had declared war on America, and they had no idea how it was being executed. But the truth wasn't that sophisticated. It was a holy war.

America was corrupt and in want of destruction. Sinners who denied Allah and refused to convert had to die. Arab children were taught that America wanted to conquer and destroy them or turn them into Christians. Children were recruited from poor religious families, trained in the desert, given minimal skills in combat, taught English and sent to America to drive cabs, work in restaurants and other unskilled labor. They were allowed to fit into American life while they waited for the call. They were required to stay in contact with Al Qaeda leaders by cell phone and through other individuals and families living in America. They were also becoming proficient in social media.

But there was also another element. There were numerous members in Al Qaeda's network who were already in America going to college or practicing medicine or in the pharmaceutical business. They were the elite and the real radicals. They didn't want to get their hands dirty, but they funneled money and passed orders down the line. They were the recruiters and manipulators. The poorer people were those who blew themselves up or sacrificed their lives for the cause. They were continually filled with rhetoric to keep them inspired. It was necessary because some of them were as much American as they were Arab. They were taught that America was evil, but in many ways they were unconvinced, even unbelieving. America had been good to them and seeing evil in a place that had given them so much was difficult.

The biggest enemy in their struggle to stay covert was the fact they were Arab and easy to spot.

Ironically, it was also their ally. In trying to appear tolerant Americans were deliberately ignoring the obvious. It was politically incorrect to insinuate that an Arab might be a radicalized Muslim. Young Arab men were allowed to go through airports unchecked while Granny was pulled out of line and searched. It was taboo to suspect five or six young Arab men of treachery when they were moving around inside a plane, changing seats and taking turns going to the washroom. It might draw the ire of the media to suspect them of being terrorists just because they were Arab. They were allowed to huddle suspiciously without drawing an inquisitive glance. Sanity had been put asunder in the name of political correctness.

They were sleeper cells, but some, as often as not were families with no more ill intentions than trying to make it in America. They thought they could use Al Qaeda to find a better life. It was just a way to get to the Promised Land. When Al Qaeda called on them, they were filled with apprehension and fear. Some of them jumped ship and found jobs in other locations and went on with their lives. Still there were plenty who would follow Al Qaeda to a suicidal end.

In recent months Al Qaeda had increasingly called upon formerly idle sleeper cells. They had a new approach. Instead of bringing down the Sears Tower or the St. Louis Arch, they would murder people on a ski slope, or kill fans at a high school basketball game, making every American family believe it could actually happen to them. Children and adults alike were put to bed in fear. The scale would be smaller but the incidents more numerous. They found financing from people like Abib. He was a small and corrupt man with a lot of money. To counter the lunacy, Anderson Claypool and the others like him had stepped up. It was a well-oiled organization and they were being fed information from the Feds. They were doing the heavy lifting in secrecy. Theirs was a war of honor, but also of revenge. Many federal law enforcement officers knew it and secretly approved of it.

Abib was driven by his hate for Americans because they thought they were better than Arabs, but deviancy was a stronger motivation than malice. Lust was his fuel and right now he wanted the blue-eyed child. The people he supported financially were dedicated to Allah, but he was in it for himself. They knew he was vile and demented and would be dead at their hands if it weren't for his money.

Sometimes when something is awry, cops from the old school get the jitters. Prosecutors call it police intuition and people within law enforcement call it "street smarts." But just as a rose is a rose by any other name, the results are the same. A good cop knows when something smells. As they sat there in the restaurant Morgan could smell it. He couldn't point it out. Maybe it was a suspicious glance, or someone turning away when he looked at them. He sensed they were under surveillance. Rudy knew it, too.

There were a lot of foreigners on the boardwalk and seeing Arab faces wasn't unusual. It was Rudy's contention that every Middle Easterner was carrying a bomb inside his underwear. Morgan's suspicions were growing. He made eye contact with one young man and it was as though time stood still. His large brown eyes were frozen like a wapiti staring into the jaws of a mountain lion. Morgan knew the man was startled. His heart pounded and his veins were gushed blood like a water cannon. Morgan had caught him. They both knew it but the man turned casually away. What was Morgan's suspicion was now a hairy little actuality.

Morgan didn't want to fear and resent Arabs. His family doctor had been from Saudi Arabia, delivered his son. He and his family were friendly, well-known, and respected in the community. There wasn't a trace of animosity, or bigotry directed towards them before 9/11. Morgan resisted preconceptions, but he had a new vent. In spite of his new slant on the Arab citizenry, this was something more than bias. It was clearly police intuition.

As they walked down the boardwalk the reality of Morgan's suspicions were growing. As quickly as storm clouds sometimes gather, trouble was closing in on him. The plastic device inside his pocket was vibrating. He took a quick glance. There were seven armed subjects at six o'clock.

"Rudy, look at this."

" That ain't good," Rudy said quietly.

Morgan slapped Jose across the shoulder with the back of his hand. "We gotta get out of here," he said in a very serious tone.

Jose didn't ask questions but followed Morgan's lead. He already trusted Morgan and Rudy to act in his best interest. He could hear the urgency in Morgan's voice and he knew something serious was coming down the pike.

Rudy visually searched the crowded boardwalk for a security guard. He had no idea what was shaking but seven men carrying heat following them was worrisome. A security guard was only a radio call away from the real police – real back-up.

Jose stepped in front of Morgan. He pointed down an alleyway. Morgan knew it was the wrong move but Jose was moving quickly. Angelique and Sonya followed him. Sonya grabbed Anna and held her close to her chest. Morgan wanted to shout, "No," but it was too late. Jose was hurrying into a trap.

Morgan's little magic block was lit up with red dots indicating armed subjects swarming his position. A GPS signal indicated two additional armed subjects approaching the opposing end of the alley. The original seven blocked the only escape route. Things were going to get nasty.

Rudy saw them coming; hurrying, reaching into their belts and jackets for 9 millimeters and 45's. He dropped to one knee to pick the 380 from his ankle holster, his hands like lead. It seemed the world had slowed down and his hands were in a creep as he grabbed at the safety strap and finally grasped the grips.

Morgan knew he was in a fight for his life. He didn't think about being retired, and he wasn't comparing himself to the young cop who wrote the book on physical fitness back in the 70's but rather the old man with tendonitis. A primal instinct to survive was let loose. His actions were all a matter of instinct now.

As the seven men approached with guns raised he grabbed the first by the throat and hit him hard with a right cross. He felt teeth crunching beneath the blow. Almost simultaneously there was a sudden jolt from the butt of a gun across his head and warm blood on his face. He staggered limply forward before he regained his balance and planted his foot and strained to stop. There was a 45 in his face. He grabbed for the hammer to prevent it from striking the loaded chamber and clutched it with all his might. He came up swinging. Another attacker went down. He could see Rudy dropping to his knee and grabbing for his 380.

Rudy's fingers were made of iron. He thought time had stopped but somehow his thumb found the safety. A young Arab man was standing over him wild-eyed, with a 45 shoved against his head. Rudy squeezed the trigger and the rapport echoed off the alley walls. Blood gushed from the man's chest as the light fled his eyes. Rudy saw a foot coming at his face, then the excruciating pain from the bone crushing blow. The light began to fade. Then it was gone.

The blood in Morgan's eyes didn't block out the sight of fists, and gun butts hammering his face and head. He could hear screaming and a child was crying.

And then it was silent. Quiet. Dark. Blank.

But then Morgan heard something. It sounded like someone was talking to him but it was his own voice. "Where am I? What happened to me?" His head throbbed and his ribs seemed to be ripping into his lungs. He couldn't focus, but red and blue lights were pulsating across his eyelids.

His mind wasn't functioning in the here and now. It was like a dream. He wondered if he was on duty, back on the job. He was confused. Had he crashed his squad car? Had he been shot? My God, he thought, Molly would be hysterical. No, I'm not a policeman, I'm retired. Where am I?"

He could see the blurred outline of someone's face. "Relax friend, you're hurt but I'm gonna take care of you. Trust me." The face faded away along with the lights and everything went dark again.

In time, light began to creep into Morgan's consciousness. The CNN News was on TV. The volume was off but a crawl was streaming across the screen. Medical reform was dead on arrival at the Senate due to the election of Scott Brown in a special election for deceased Senator Edward Kennedy's seat in Massachusetts.

"Right," Morgan mumbled. "Those Dems will ride that medical reform right into a Republican landslide in November."

"Where am I?"

He ran his hand down the stainless steel bedrail. Nurses in green scrubs crossed the doorway. There was a clear plastic tube attached to a needle in his arm and a drip bag over his head. He glanced around the room and saw Rudy in a bed a few feet away. His vision was blurred but he could see that Rudy had one eye closed and the other focused on him. His face was battered and bruised.

"What the heck happened?" Rudy asked.

"I don't know. The last thing I remember we were sitting at Nick's." Morgan said.

They were both quiet as they tried to recall the events leading them to their hospital beds.

"Angelique," Morgan whispered. "She was with us." It was starting to come back to him now.

"We were beaten into the dirt, Morgan," Rudy said. He was quiet for a while as he contemplated the situation. "I think I shot a man," he said.

"I think you're right. Everything is still foggy, but I think we messed up. We should have gone to the FBI."

"What happened to Angelique, Sonya, and Jose – and the little girl?"

"I don't know."

Slowly, incrementally all the details soaked in. They had been jumped and left unconscious in an alley. They had to assume they were discovered and transported to the hospital by ambulance. There was a uniformed police officer sitting in a chair outside their hospital room. It was logical to conclude that there was also a dead body found along with them. Rudy remember gazing into the man's eyes when the light went out of them. He was as dead as a hammer as far as Rudy was concerned.

As they coped with their pain and bemoaned their dilemma, a large athletic black man strolled down the hallway towards their room. He stopped and talked briefly with the policeman at the door. After only a moment he stepped into the room.

"Well, what's all dis? Who dat in dease beds," He said in a heavy southern black drawl.

"Ah, crap," Rudy sighed.

"You sho is a sorry look'n couple a Yankee crackers," he said.

"Hello, Anderson," Morgan said.

"What's up?" Anderson said.

"We've run into a little bad luck. Some other stuff too."

"You mean stuff like Angelique Sanchez, Sonya Isles and a few soulless Arab who steal American girls and take them to Saudi Arabia?" The accent was gone. He wore a vague little smile.

Morgan and Rudy glanced at each other.

"I've got some things to tell you, too, but it's going to take a while, so I think we need to find another location to talk.

Just at that moment Thelma stepped through the doorway and slid a black bag across the floor. Anderson picked it up and opened it. Inside there was a change of clothing for both Morgan and Rudy. There was a small black case, and a clear plastic bag containing Rudy's 380.

"We can't go anywhere. We're laid up bad," Morgan grimaced. "And if you haven't noticed, there's a policeman sitting outside our door."

"Yeah, he probably wants you to stay here until the detectives have a chance to talk to you."

"Rudy killed one of the guys who jumped us," Morgan said.

"There wasn't a dead man there when the police arrived."

"How do you know?"

"I know things," Anderson said.

Anderson opened the black bag and retrieved a needle and syringe. He flicked it with his middle finger as he depressed the plunger to remove the air inside the glass tube. This will make you feel a lot better," he said.

"Are you a doctor?" Rudy asked through a moan. "I mean besides your job as a doorman for Harmon Edison."

"No."

"How do you know what that stuff will do to us?"

"It'll make you better or it'll kill you," Anderson said.

"I'm not take'n it," Rudy said.

"Yes, you are," Anderson said, as he stabbed the needle into Rudy's arm. Rudy flinched and waited breathlessly for the blankness of death. In only a moment he was feeling better. Anderson reached into the bag and flipped a pair of pants and a polo shirt to Rudy. "It's not quite up to the level of the Memphis Zoo shirts you've been wearing, but it'll do."

Morgan got a shot and he was feeling better too. "What about the cop at the door?"

"He's taking a nap."

Morgan glanced at the doorway. The policeman was slumped in his chair.

"Thelma gave him a little nightcap."

"Who are you? You're sure not some dumb security guard." Morgan said firmly.

"I'm a man who has a job to do, and you're going to help me, so get dressed."

In only a few moments they were getting into a black Chevy at the emergency room exit. Thelma drove without speaking.

"Take us to Hollywood Beach," Anderson said. Both Morgan and Rudy had broken ribs, contusions, and abrasions, but neither of them had serious head injuries. They struggled to the car and just like that they were ex-patients.

In less than an hour they were all sitting at Nick's in the outside dining area. Anderson told them as much as he could without placing himself in jeopardy. Being police officers Morgan and Rudy knew when to stop asking questions. Sometimes it's better not to know the details. It's called taking a non-accountability position. The less you know, the less you have to give up under oath. For Anderson, it was more like "If I told you, I'd have to kill you."

Now it was their task to watch the passing tourists for faces to match those of their attackers. Anderson believed if they found even one of them he could extract enough information to find Angelique and the others. It was important for Anderson to rescue them. It was that one lonely link to his humanity.

The afternoon languidly drug on without a clue. When the pain returned Rudy petitioned for another shot of the medicine. Anderson shot them up again but warned them that they would have to suffer through their pain if it returned. The substance he was giving them was Oxycontin which was worse than being deadly. It was an evil monster capable of swallowing the willpower of men and leaving them dependent and broken.

In the quiet and empty Majestic Hotel, Pedro and Maria busied themselves carrying potted plants from the lobby to locations on each of the 12 floors. Fresh paint and new carpet smells filled the air. Sometimes they moved plants from one location to another trying to look busy when there was nothing constructive left to do. Losing the gig at the Majestic wasn't a foregone conclusion so they were faking productivity to impress the owner. Although he had told them that they would have to go once the hotel was open, they were holding out for a permanent position. Pedro thought he might be the groundskeeper and Maria could work in the laundry. Since neither of them spoke English it was hard to get it across to the owner how badly they wanted to stay. They would work hard for less and work for cash. They just didn't know how to say it.

They were ordered to stay off the top floor, but in an effort to show their eagerness to please they were there anyway, potting plants and distributing fresh flowers. No comprendo was an easy out.

Pedro was on his knees shoving soil into a clay pot

to secure a sago palm. Maria was standing over him volunteering her expertise. The elevator door opened and several young Arab men stepped off. Pedro glanced up, Maria turned her back pretending to be busy arranging flowers. There were two women, a Hispanic man, and a little girl with them being guided along. Maria watched them in a mirror on the wall. The door opened into Abib's apartment and all but one of them went inside. He lingered in the hallway studying Pedro and Maria. Finally he approached Pedro, stood over him, and stared at him for a long moment. Pedro continued to dig in the clay pot. When he looked up, the man glared at him. Pedro smiled and said, "Beunos dios, Amigo." With that said the man slowly walked up the hallway, occasionally glancing over his shoulder suspiciously until he entered Abib's suite.

Morgan, Rudy and Anderson were seated in the open air dining area at Nick's, still examining the faces of people as they walked by. The aroma of veal and roasted garlic simmering in butter lingered in the air. Morgan could have been hungry, but the thought of chewing was too painful for him to seriously consider eating. Rudy swallowed a few meatballs in spite of his discomfort. Anderson ate a salad and drank a few ounces of red wine, but he was focused on the tourists, never allowing his attention to wander away from the task at hand. He frequently pointed to prospective individuals in the crowd and asked Morgan and Rudy to look at them. Neither were ready to give up, but as time ticked away it was getting harder to recall the faces.

Down the boardwalk, tourists began to part like a wave splitting around a buoy. Morgan watched the commotion and then Pedro and Maria emerged, trotting along with their little fists clenched, and their features set in determination. Pedro's eyes were locked on Morgan's face as if he knew just where he would find him. They slid to a stop like cartoon characters. They were breathing heavily, waving their arms and talking rapidly in Spanish.

Rudy interrupted them, holding up an open hand, "Stop."

They zipped it instantly, but their faces were full of anxiety.

"Surely you understand Spanish," Rudy remarked to Anderson.

Anderson did not speak Spanish. Although he seemed to have superman qualities in many respects he responded that he had taken French in high school and college, not a word of Spanish.

Rudy grimaced, "You can see through walls, but you can't speak Spanish?"

"Shut it, Rudopp, we need to find out what they're trying to tell us. It may be important."

Maria stood before them, exasperated at the lack of communication. She looked at Morgan for several seconds with her eyes bearing down on him like little black dots. Finally she blurted out, "Jose Garcia." Only fate would have it that Maria still thought that Morgan and Rudy were looking to apprehend Jose.

Anderson was instantly on his feet. Morgan and Rudy were slower to respond, but amazingly quick for their deteriorated conditions. Anderson grabbed Maria's hand and drug her through the crowd. He looked up and down the boardwalk. He wasn't frantic but more so a man on a mission. Finally he saw what he was looking for in Sorrento's Restaurant. A Mexican waiter poured water for a middle-aged couple. Surely he believed it was the Grim Reaper as Anderson descended upon him. He shrunk away as Anderson hulked over him. Maria was dangling like a rag doll.

"Do you speak English? Anderson demanded.

"Si! Yes, I mean."

"You're bi-lingual?"

"Yes, yes, I do. I am."

Anderson's hand came upon the waiter's arm in one swift movement. He was pulled along as a toddler might be whisked away by an angry mother. His water pitcher exploded when it hit the floor. Like a puppet careening along, his feet ricocheted across the ground. He glanced over his shoulder with a puzzled and panicked expression.

The manager hustled out to investigate. "What the hell's going on?" he shouted.

Rudy reached feebly into his back pocket and retrieved his badge case. He dangled his badge as he followed Anderson, marching along with Maria and the waiter at his mercy. "We need him for police business. We'll bring him back."

The manager watched in disbelief as Rudy limped out the doorway. With all the bandages and bloody blotches seeping through them, he looked like he was playing the Mummy at the amphitheater.

"It must be rough police business," the manager muttered to himself.

Chapter Twenty Three

Raja Kahn was getting nervous. He and his Arab companions were only a few miles out of Boynton Beach. He knew how to drive a semi; that was one of the reasons he had been chosen for this operation. Pretending to be Ajiith Aswami was getting easier. Ajiith had been a sleeper cell driver. In retrospect, learning how to park semis at the terminal lot had been his misfortune. Without the ability to drive an eighteen-wheeler he might have lived to a ripe old age. Ajiith went into Al Qaeda shortly after the Oklahoma City bombing. By the devastating results the truck bomb had on the Edward Morrow building the method was immediately adopted by Al Qaeda. They needed drivers for big trucks for that kind of a job. The idea of stuffing a semi-trailer full of combatants to move them secretly from one location to another was a natural expansion of the original idea. Hence, Ajiith's involvement. As a result Anderson had emptied Ajiith's brains into a red hand towel and jammed his body into the trunk of a car. Where he was at that moment, only Anderson knew.

A nervous Raja had made up his mind that he wasn't going anywhere near Hollywood Beach with a semi-truck full of murderers. He would find a ravine deep enough to do some real damage and drive the truck into it. He was full of angst. He didn't want to die. He wanted desperately to live, but he wasn't going to stand by and let Yellow Eyes create a blood wave onto the beach. Where was that Godforsaken Anderson?!

Anderson, Rudy, Morgan and their true-hearted little Mexican friends, along with the abducted waiter were under the canopy at the amphitheater. Anderson waited, occasionally calmly checking his watch as he listened to the story Pedro and Maria were telling. When he had all the details he reached into Rudy's pocket and plucked out his badge case. He flashed it at the waiter for a split second, not long enough for the waiter to read it. "Have you got a green card?" he asked sternly.

"No, Amigo, I don't."

"Are you a citizen?"

"No."

"Then get the out of here! And if you tell anyone about what just happened, you'll be back in Mexico before you can spit. You savvy?"

"Si!"

With that said, the waiter disappeared into the stream of tourists on the boardwalk.

"What do you think those s daemon will do with them?" Morgan asked.

"They'll probably kill the older woman. The young woman and her child will go to Saudi Arabia. The man will be used in a terrorist video."

"What kind of video?" Rudy asked.

"What kind do you think? They'll dope him up, put him on his knees in front of the camera, force him to denounce America, then cut off his head. They'll start from the back of the neck so the blood trickles into the throat. They want the screams to be accentuated by the gurgling of blood."

"Don't say anymore. I saw the video of that Jewish kid being murdered a few years back. I couldn't sleep for a week," Rudy said.

"We gotta do something," Morgan snapped.

"Go get the guns The Jesus impersonator dumped on you and the GPS that was with them." Anderson ordered.

Morgan wasn't concerned about the impersonator or about why the guns were dumped on them. It was curious, but the urgency of the situation didn't allow for explanations. He was only interested in getting the guns and getting into action. Anderson handed Rudy the .380 with a newly-installed silencer attached. Rudy didn't ask him how he got it back from the Police Department. He tucked it in his belt.

Morgan handed the black plastic block to Anderson. "That's it, the GPS thing." he said.

"I'll meet you near the Majestic Hotel. Let's get going."

Pedro and Maria obediently followed Morgan and Rudy. "You need to find a safe place and stay there," Morgan said. They just looked at him. "I mean it, go – vamoose!"

They stood their ground, confused but as loyal as a couple of lap dogs.

"Go Pedro, scram!"

Pedro adamantly refused, insisting that they would go with him. His words were part English and part Spanish and what he said was unintelligible, but Morgan got it. Pedro and Maria were going with them, and that was that!

"Come on, then," Morgan said, "but Maria stays here!"

They hurried off to get the Heckler machine guns.

In moments they were back with the canvas bag with the machine guns and the 9-millimeter clips, also now equipped with silencers. Two police officers meandered past them as they hurried towards the Majestic. Morgan had a sense of detachment as he considered all the madness. One of the police officers glanced at them without the slightest concern. They were carrying illegal weapons in plain sight, but it didn't even elicit a second look. They were beat up and bandaged, obviously out of place, but they went undetected through the crowd. There were murderers who were going to propel an innocent child into a life of sexual servitude, kill a hard-working gentle woman, and cut off the head of a man who had done nothing to them. Still the wind was gently streaming off the ocean, children were laughing and chasing waves, and tourists from all walks of life were complacently relaxing in the sun. Everything seemed so normal. Who would possibly guess what was happening? It was insanity! Why wouldn't he be contacting the FBI right at that very moment.

He should have done just that, but he couldn't. He had become a part of it. They were involved. He and Rudy were huffing for air as they hustled to get back to their meeting place. Anderson was waiting. As huge as a black granite monument he stood with determination in his eyes, fearless, and ready to press on.

Morgan handed the canvass bag to him and he

opened it and retrieved the guns. There were numerous casual glances at them as they loaded the clips into the guns and readied themselves for battle, but no one gave them a serious look. It was as though anything that audacious couldn't actually be real.

"We have to make quick work of this. I've got something really menacing coming down in short order," Anderson said.

Morgan was aghast. "What could be more critical than this?"

"You'll know soon enough. Let's go," Anderson snorted.

With that said, Pedro led them to the servants' entrance. They marched past the empty service desk to catch the main elevator to the 12th floor. Morgan's heart pounded and his lips were parched like a man who had the misfortune of spending the night unprepared in the desert.

"I'm beat up and stiff, but mostly I'm scared, Morg" Rudy whispered to Morgan.

Morgan nodded.

They took the elevator to the 11th floor. Anderson was first to exit. Quick glances in all directions confirmed that the hallway was clear but Anderson already knew in advance because of the little black plastic block of infinite datum. He stopped and analyzed the device, signaled for the others to follow as he headed for the stairwell. Morgan had one of the Hecklers and Anderson had the other. Rudy was ready with his .380.

"Do you know how to use that thing?" Anderson pointed to the Heckler.

"Yes."

There must have been a little doubt in his eyes because Anderson calmly reached over and flipped the safety switch to the off position. A fourteen-shot clip was in position. Morgan had two others stuck in his belt.

"You point it and pull the trigger." Anderson said.

"Right," Morgan whispered.

"Give one of the clips in your belt to Rudy. If you go down he can pick up the Heckler and get back into the fight."

Time stopped. Morgan and Rudy looked at each other. The fear was palpable, but deeper in the exchange, true appreciation and brotherhood was heavy and unspoken. "Good luck, old friend," radiated in a melancholy meeting of their eyes.

"This is a war," Anderson snapped. "We didn't start it, it came to us. Our government is too gutless to fight our enemies so we have to do it. So, just like soldiers in any war we have to put ourselves on the line. Get your mean look on and let's get those bastards!"

His attitude gave them courage. Pedro didn't understand a word of it but he was pacing with his fist clinched, eyebrows furrowed in condemnation. Morgan and Rudy both snapped to attention. They both gave Anderson a quick affirmative head nod. They were ready.

Anderson opened the doorway and started up the stairwell three steps at a time. Morgan's knees were aching, his ribs throbbing, and the tendons in his shoulders were burning but he remained on Anderson's tail. Rudy was struggling as fast as his sturdy old frame would carry him.

They hit the hallway running. Anderson approached Abib's suite. He kicked the doorway in full stride. Splinters and pieces of the door exploded into the air. Anderson filled the doorway blocking Morgan's view of the room's interior, but he heard a burst of three shots from Anderson's Heckler.

Once Anderson had vacated the doorway, Morgan saw a young Arab lying in the floor, blood gushing from his chest.

The huge room was occupied with a lot of overstuffed furniture. There was a tripod and video camera pointing towards a wall where a gray tarp had been hung. There was a man on his knees with a canvass bag over his head. He was crumpled as though he had collapsed. Without seeing a face Morgan knew it was Jose.

Those bastards!

Three men rushed down the hallway carrying machine guns. Anderson took out the first two, released his clip, grabbed for another and slipped it rapidly into his gun. The third man was pointing his gun at Anderson's head as he entered the room. Morgan pulled his trigger.

Picture frames and vases disintegrated as a spray of bullets pounded the room. Man number three was hit in his arm, but he was still moving towards Anderson. With one swift movement Anderson lunged forward and grabbed his throat. In an instant, his eyes bulged their sockets and blood frothed from his mouth.

Pedro raced across the room in the midst of the gunfire and found Angelique, Sonya, and Anna. All were bound and tied. Frantically he cut at the ropes and duct tape with his pocketknife. Sonya grabbed Anna and covered her with her body.

Anderson checked the GPS and then started down the hallway. There were still four men in the suite He entered the master bedroom and a short burst from the Heckler left another man lifeless.

Rudy found his way to a media room where one of the men was circling frantically trying to find a way out. Rudy confronted him. He wasn't a soldier, he was a policeman. His first instinct was to apprehend the man. "Halt!" he shouted.

His answer came in the form of gunfire, erratic and untrained. Walls and furniture were shredded into pieces, but Rudy was left standing. Rudy turned sideways and pulled his arms in close to cover his heart as he had been taught. He aimed at his attacker and emptied the .380 into him. The man was dead before he hit the floor.

That left two. One of the men came down the hallway with his hands cupped behind his head. "Don't shoot, don't shoot!" he shouted. His English was perfect.

Anderson ran at him with rage in his eyes. His teeth were clenched in hatred. He hit him in the chest with his broad shoulder and flipped him into the air. Even before he hit the floor Anderson was on him like a lion going for the kill. The man was on his back but with one fluid motion Anderson turned him onto his stomach and grabbed his head and started to wrench it backwards. Anderson's strength would have taken one well-placed heave to loosen the man's head from his neck.

Morgan instantly grabbed Anderson to restrain him from killing him.

"Anderson, he surrendered!"

"Forget that that!" Anderson shouted.

"It's murder, Anderson. It's murder!"

Anderson looked around the room as though searching for something.

Sonya was holding Anna. Her eyes were wide in anticipation, revealing her willingness to watch. There was no expression of sympathy or plea for mercy.

Angelique was with Jose. He was alive! Her focus was solely to care for him. The man who tortured Jose only moments ago was now begging for his life.

Angelique disengaged. She didn't care what happened to him.

Anderson lessened his grip, but not enough for the man to feel anything less than excruciating pain. He struggled for air and moaned incoherently. Anderson sat atop him like a man riding a fence rail. Anderson was as fit as a human body could be, a rock. The activity so far wouldn't have caused him to break a sweat, but he heaved for air as if he had run a two-mile sprint. The internal battle was still being waged. He was trying to pull himself back from the brink into the realm of humanity. He restrained himself with every muscle in his body. He wasn't an animal. That would, indeed, be a blessing for Anderson at this moment. Animals fought for survival. But when the battle was won, they moved on. He wanted that, but it wasn't to be. How could he forget and move on? What about Angie and the twins? How could they move on?

"I'm going to kill this Patel," he snarled.

Just at that moment Abib ran into the room. He was pathetic and desperate as he headed for the door. The hunter had now become the hunted. His billions were worthless to him. His fate was already in the bag. His battle was lost and an uncontrollable whimpering escaped his lips. His frenzied attempt to flee was replaced by the frank realization of the situation and then utter hopelessness. He was waving a 9 millimeter wildly as his body lunged for the door.

Rudy and Morgan began to close in on him when he let loose with a volley of bullets from the handgun. Morgan pointed the machine gun and fired. Abib was riddled with lead. He hit the floor with eyes fixed wide open. The degenerate was given into the hands of Satan.

Morgan stood over Abib, waiting for him to move; waiting for him to say that he was injured but just needed to get to the hospital. Morgan's mind not able to comprehend what had just happened yet. He had been a policeman for 28 years. Service to people was his first priority. He had never killed a man. He didn't want that burden, not even this human cauldron of evil.

He didn't have to contemplate his actions long. Sonya raced across the room and fell to her knees in front of Anderson. Blood poured from a gash in his neck.

Rudy inched near to him slowly, stunned. He couldn't believe his eyes. It was incomprehensible for Superman to be lying in a pool of blood. Rudy became suspended in his tracks. Anderson was helpless on the floor, struggling for his next breath. Sonya had covered the wound with her bare hands and the blood was rushing between her fingers. He was hit when Abib sprayed the room with random fire.

Anderson was a mighty bull who had been

skewered. He seemed invincible but now he was human and down, slowly fading away. The quiet was deafening. The man Anderson had in his throes was dead. Anderson's last function was to snap a man's neck like a pretzel. Now, Abib lay motionless beside Anderson with Anderson's blood soaking into his clothing.

They were both killers. One killed for a distorted religious doctrine, and the other for revenge. Soon they would be equals in death as surely as judgment would ring out in the hereafter.

Anderson whispered Morgan's name. Sonya called for him and Morgan sunk to his knees beside him. He pressed his ear close in order to hear. Anderson struggled with his words, but he was able to say everything he needed to say.

Anderson hurriedly related the details of the pending disaster for Hollywood Beach. He got Morgan's pledge to help, and then closed his eyes. Anderson's agony was over.

"Via con Dios," Pedro said softly.

Morgan looked panicked. " Rudy, we have to go."

"Where?"

"Let's go! Let's go! Go, go, go!" He was clearly panicked about what Anderson had said. .

"What about all this?" he asked.

"We have to go, all of us," Morgan shouted, waving his arms.

Rudy turned and took one last look at Anderson as he followed Morgan from the room. The total horror of the scene smacked him in the face. The others trailed behind him.

Jose was regaining his strength, but he needed help from Angelique and Sonya. Anna was wide-eyed and completely withdrawn. As they hurried down the boardwalk they resembled an entourage from a horror movie. Morgan and Rudy were bandaged and limping. Sonya was covered with Anderson's blood, and Jose was swaying and suffering from having been drugged, bound and beaten. Pedro and Maria prayed aloud.

People watched them as they journeyed down the brick pavers towards the parking garage. Their stares were curious but detached; not motivated by concern.

When they reached Rudy's car everyone was exhausted. Morgan ordered Angelique and Sonya to go to the Sea Breeze and stay there. Maria tried to get in the car with them, but Morgan firmly nixed it.

"If an older woman by the name of Thelma comes looking for us, tell her where she can find Anderson. Tell her that we need help. Tell her I have the black box."

There wasn't time to explain where he was going. They had to get moving.

With that said Morgan, Rudy and Pedro were off. Angelique, Sonya, Anna and Maria were left behind wondering.

Morgan was driving as they hit the toll way north to I-95, driving like a man with his hair on fire. As he weaved into and out of traffic, he explained that there was a transfer truck full of terrorist headed for Hollywood Beach. One of the occupants was an agent working with Anderson. He had a credit card sized GPS in his wallet that would enable them to find them. When they were in range the GPS in the plastic block would be activated.

Once they found the semi, they had to stop it.

Rudy was beyond nervous, dumbfounded. "This is like one of those movies where shootouts happen in plain sight and dead bodies are left all over the place, but the police never come. Midway through his thought process, Rudy said, "This ain't a movie, Morg, this is us. Is this really happening, or is this some crazy nightmare?"

"Rudy, we don't have any choices. There's a truck load of murderers on their way to Hollywood Beach to kill everybody there!"

"We can't do this, Morg. Anderson had help. He had an organization. Hell, we don't even know how to contact Thelma."

"We have to try, Rudy."

"What are we gonna do with a truck full of murderers!"

"We have to find them first!"

"And then they kill us, right?"

As they burned the pavement northbound on I-95 Morgan weighed his options. They could call the FBI or the Florida State Police. He knew the system well enough to know that the first response from them would be to suspect they were a couple of screwballs. Once they questioned them thoroughly and found there was validity to their claim, bodies would already be flayed and bleeding on the beach.

There was only one option. He had to find a way to stop them by himself; he, Rudy and Pedro.

At that moment Raja Kahn was southbound out of Boynton Beach. The semi- trailer was crammed with Arab men. Most of the part-time combatants were in their twenties. They were students, clerks, gas station attendants, and convenient mart owners. Some of them were illegal immigrants, but most were naturalized and homegrown U.S citizens. They were all Muslims.

Yellow Eyes was in the truck cab with Raja. He was quiet and focused. He was satisfied with the plan. He knew that recently Al Qaeda had failed in Fisher, Indiana, Nederland, Colorado, and a little town in Alabama. He knew Al Qaeda had connections within the FBI that would enable him to eventually learn why, but at the moment it was still a mystery as to what happened.

He had lost contact with Abib earlier in the afternoon, and that worried him, but constant contact was the exception, not the rule. Still this was a good plan.

Anyone who was not born in the modern era would not be able to conceive the insanity of terrorism. In all of history there had never been anything so absurd. Murdering innocent people to create fear for political gains had been in existence since mankind became upright, but never on the scale of the late twentieth century and the early twenty first.

The inhumanity was unbelievable. Cutting off someone's head to make a point; hell, nobody would do that, would they? How crazy is that? Still they do it. Still they kill innocent children who have done nothing worse than to breathe the air. Arab children, Iranian children, Iraqi children, and Saudi Arabian children are blown to pieces in the streets because Muslims hate America. It is crazy, but regretfully true.

So this was a good plan. Yellow Eyes and his misled platoon of murderers were en route to Hollywood Beach to kill as many unsuspecting people as they were able to kill. When they were finished they would release deadly chemicals into the air to polish off the rest of them. It was a peachy idea. When it was all said and done, they would be no closer to bringing down America than they were when they started. They would only be a step closer to their own annihilation

.   Raja Kahn was an all American boy. The only thing he had in common with the others was the color of his skin and the sound of his name. He believed in America. He didn't really know anything about the economies or lifestyles of the Middle Eastern countries. He had a good life as an American. Nobody had ever treated him with contempt or exposed him to racial hatred until America was attacked by Arabs. He totally understood it. He wanted revenge as much as any other red-blooded American, maybe even more. His parents, too, died in the 9/11 attack.

The only problem with revenge and heroism from Raja's vantage point was that he was standing on death's door. If Anderson Claypool failed to show up, he was diving headfirst into the grave.

Anderson Claypool was dead. Morgan Cooper, Rudy Campbell, and loyal-to-a-fault Pedro were his stand-ins. Raja Kahn and the fate of every tourist at Hollywood Beach were now in the hands of two retired small town cops and an illegal immigrant. Nobody in the mix had drawn a winning hand!

Morgan was cruising north on I-95 when the locator indicated they had found their target. Before Anderson died he had given Morgan the details he needed to identify the semi-truck and the U-Hall trailer. Once the GPS indicated the position, he would be able to eyeball the right vehicle. Arrogantly, it carried a huge Star of David decal on the trailer doors. How absurd was that?

As the indicator beeped, Morgan hit the exit at 87 miles per hour. The tires were screeching, blue smoke bellowed as they skidded and swerved.

"Dammit, Morgan. I don't wanna die before the terrorist get the chance to kill me!" Rudy snickered.

Morgan laughed nervously. There was nothing funny about the situation, but if Rudy was going to try to overcome his fear with humor, the least Morgan could do was laugh. Strangely, it helped to release some of the tension. He had been on rewind in his thought, "Everybody has to die sometime."

So far it hadn't mitigated the thought of it. Humor seemed to work better.

Just as they crossed the overpass to make the return onto the interstate southbound, the semi bearing the Star of David was passing beneath them, being accompanied by a Mercedes pulling a U-Haul. Morgan goosed the Lincoln and passed a van carrying a load of children. Because there was only one lane on the exit ramp, the van was forced onto the roadside. The woman who was driving honked and shouted angrily as they sped away. Morgan weaved in and out of traffic until he was able to fall in behind the U-Haul.

Within sight there was a Florida State Police car parked in the median. The letters across the rear window read K-9 Unit. The trooper was running radar, but it was likely he was watching for drug runners as well.

"I've got an idea," Rudy shouted, reaching for his cell phone. He dialed 911. In seconds the 911 operator was on the line. Rudy frantically reported a drunken driver in a silver Mercedes pulling a U-Haul trailer, knowing that when he made the report that the trooper in the median was close and would respond to the call.

"That sniffer dog will hit on them chemicals in the U-Haul," he said.

Morgan sounded his approval, "good thinking, Rudy."

In moments the state car was closing on them with red and blue lights flashing. Morgan changed lanes to allow the police car to take position behind the U-Haul. It slowed to pull over to the curb. As Morgan went around them he made eye contact with the passenger. Fear and panic bled from his face, not the steely-eyed murderous expression he expected to see. With that expression he might as well have posted a Terrorist on Board sign in the window.

"That's three down and 61 to go," Rudy said.

Morgan moved up on the semi, which had slowed down considerably as a result of the U-Haul being pulled over. Morgan only hoped that the three men in the Mercedes would play it cool, holding out for something no more serious than a traffic violation. If they panicked they would probably open gunfire. If they did that the state trooper would be toast, another image for Morgan and Rudy to carry to their graves. If the dog hit on the chemicals before he found himself in jeopardy he could get into combat position and call for backup. Morgan hoped for the latter, but regardless, it was a risk they had to take.

He, Rudy, and Pedro were in ever deepening hot water, but getting the U-Haul out of the way was a small victory.

The semi was indicating a turn onto the off

ramp. Morgan guessed they were getting off the highway to investigate what had happened to the U-Haul. Thinking as much like a terrorist as he could muster, Morgan theorized they were preparing a contingency plan. If they weren't surrounded by police cars in a few moments they would continue on to Hollywood Beach and complete their treachery. If the cops came they would make a stand right where they were. They would kill as many cops as they could and then start on passing motorist. After all they were terrorists - creating terror and tumult was their purpose.

The semi turned into the Floradixie Truck Stop. It was the largest trucker haven in Florida. There were trucks and trailers parked row upon row in the parking lot, still idling while the drivers were in the restaurant and drivers' lounge. A hefty cluster of Harley Davidson motorcycles were aligned near the front entrance. If there was one redneck there, there were a hundred.

"Is that log chain still in the trunk? The one the bobcat driver used to pull us out of the ditch?" Morgan asked, not going into further detail.

Rudy thought it was there, but his mind was so occupied with the tentative situation he couldn't answer anything directly.

Morgan stopped at the curb while Rudy was quick to go to the trunk to retrieve the log chain. He didn't ask for an explanation. Morgan was doing all the thinking now. Morgan slid into the passenger seat and ordered Rudy to drive. In a few moments they were behind the semi again. It slowed to a stop between two parked semi-trailers. Morgan jumped from the front seat with the log chain in tow. He had forgotten about his broken ribs and battered body. Like a cat, his age and fatigue on hold, he wrapped the log chain around the trailer door latch securing it in the locked position. He hurried back to the car. The men inside the semi-trailer were now locked in.

"Where's your 380, Rudy?" he asked.

Rudy didn't answer. He just shoved it into Morgan's hand. Morgan checked the clip and the silencer. It was ready to go.

"Get those Hecklers ready. If those fuckers break out of that trailer door, shoot 'em down!"

"I will," Rudy said obediently. Pedro grabbed the guns and pitched one to Rudy.

Morgan edged up close to the rear semi-trailer wheels. He sneaked alongside the truck until he was crouched beside the truck passenger door. His heart was pounding the sound of blood was pumping in his ears. "Everybody has to die sometime," he said softly.

In just a split second he was on the running board of the semi. He grabbed the door handle and jerked open the door. Suddenly he was eyeball to eyeball with Yellow Eyes. He shoved the gun against his head and pulled the trigger. Those yellow eyes rolled back inside their sockets and his head snapped forward. Blood and brain spewed into the air as his skull popped like a rotten melon. The driver sat stunned.

"What's your name?" Morgan shouted.

"Raja Kahn! I'm American!"

"What's the phrase? What are you supposed to say," Morgan demanded.

Raja was frozen in fear. He stuttered and stammered. "I, I, ah."

"Say it or I'll blow your brains out!"

216

"What do you mean – what do you want me to say"

"Only two people know that phrase. Anderson killed one of them. If you don't spill it, I'll kill you!"

Somehow in the midst of the fear and confusion Raja realized that Morgan wanted the proverb.

"Let me think, let me think!"

"You've got about ten seconds!" Morgan shouted.

"It's not the – It's not the - God help me think! Dwell not upon they weariness, the measure of the strength - mannnn! Dwell not upon thy weariness, the measure of thy…." Raja was exasperated.

"That's good enough," Morgan said, sighing deeply. It wasn't quite right but it would do. His respite was short-lived. There were still 60 murderers stuck in the semi van. If they hadn't already discovered they were locked in, it was only a matter of time until they did. Morgan surmised that once they found they were captive the hot lead would be heading their direction. He and Raja stuffed Yellow Eyes into the sleeper cab to block the gunfire when it started.

Rudy waited with his eyes fixed on the semi-trailer doors. He was counting the minutes to the end of his life. He regretted not having one more occasion with a woman. He was going to take as many terrorists with him as he could. His death watch was interrupted when Morgan exited the truck cab and came back to the car. He quickly updated Rudy on the situation. "Yellow Eyes is dead. The man who was driving the truck was Raja Kahn, Anderson's associate." All others were Muslim radicals.

There was little doubt about the seriousness of the

217

matter. They were probably going to die if they didn't flee. They decided together that they would die like men. Still Morgan had a plan. It was simple and everything hinged on pure unadulterated luck. They talked it over and agreed to go for it.

They had a chance if it worked.

Morgan ran for the truck cab. The sixty men in the van were shouting and kicking against the thin metal semi-trailer walls. They had figured out there was a wrinkle in their plans. It would be only moments before the ammo would be rattling the metal siding, deafening its occupants.

He jumped back into the passenger seat. "Hit it, Raja!" His new companion shoved the gearshift forward and gunned the engine. The truck bucked and surged forward. The 60 men in the trailer were caught off guard when the weight shifted and they were thrown against the trailer doors and mashed together like sardines in a can. They were quiet as they shuffled and shifted around to regain their footing. Back on their feet they were again shouting and kicking at the door and trailer siding.

Suddenly gunfire erupted. Yellow Eyes was being riddled with lead. The dead body was bouncing and lunging as though he had been wound up on a spring. The metal from the truck cab and the dead body were stopping the shells from getting through, but sooner or later bullets would be tearing through the body mass and filling the truck cab.

"Turn here and take it in front of the driver's lounge," Morgan shouted. Raja cut the wheels in the direction of the restaurant as a cloud of dust followed him. As the roar of the machine gunfire covered every inch of the sleeper cab, Raja floored the accelerator and the truck sped into the main parking lot.

Rudy's Lincoln slid to a stop. He and Pedro jumped from the car and headed for the double glass doors. Rudy was limping as he burst through the doorway with his retired police badge at the end an extended arm.

The restaurant was full of truck drivers with big bellies, huge cowboy belt buckles and John Deere baseball caps. They were bearded and furry, unkempt and worn from days on the road. Additionally, there were the Harley riders sporting orange and black t-shirts, black leather vests with Old Glory, proudly displayed across their backs. If one would have shouted, "God bless American," the "Amens", and "you better believe it," would have rocked the house. Most of them were visibly carrying heat. If they didn't have a gun somewhere on their person, there was a sawed off shotgun behind the seat in the cab of the truck.

Rudy rammed his way through the crowded room like a bulldozer, bashing tables and knocking truckers over like bowling pins. Both he and Pedro stood there with the Heckler machine guns dangling at their sides.

"We need help! There's terrorists outside trying to kill us all!" Rudy bellowed.

The room went silent. There was some shuffling and scooting of chairs as people aligned themselves to see what was happening. Some of them reached inside their coats for their own guns, nervous about weapons Rudy and Pedro were holding.

"The parking lot is full of terrorist, Goddammit, I

219

mean it! We need help!" Rudy yelled. Pedro was jumping like a little imp into the air pointing into the parking lot. Boots were shuffling across the floor as truckers and Harley riders moved around to take a peek. The semi came sliding to a stop directly in front of the broad window where booths lined the wall. Bullets pierced the trailer walls and soon the restaurant windows were being riddled with holes. The restaurant patrons who hadn't taken Rudy seriously were now holding their asses and diving for the floor. The people in the booths had slipped under their tables. When the glass shattered and crashed onto the sidewalk Raja hauled away from the building and stopped in the open parking lot. Hot lead and smoke poured out of the semi van with a vengeance.

In an instant, truckers, bikers, and motorists were swarming out the doors and scrambling for their vehicles like a nest of hornets. It was as if a premixed barrel of rage and fury was discharged into the air where it was absorbed into the mob as they readied for battle.

Anger had been festering for eleven years and now the lid was about to blow. A few shots were fired into the side of the trailer by men who were toting handguns. Double-barreled shotgun blasts roared and the metal on the trailer was torn like paper. If the terrorists inside the trailer didn't know before that their sinister plans had been disrupted, they knew it when the buckshot tore gigantic holes through the trailer siding. The Harley riders were loaded with heat but many of the truckers had to go to their rides to retrieve their irons. As truck doors were slammed shut, the parking lot began to rock with gunfire.

The back door of the semi van was finally broken through and Arabs were diving out onto the ground. Some of them hit the asphalt running, but others were picked right out of the air like clay pigeons. It was a spectacle likened to a Chinese fireworks festival. The flashes from the gunfire lit up the parking lot as the entire area sizzled like severed utility wires snapping, writhing and breathing lightning bolts.

Rudy merely stood with the Heckler machine gun dangling at his side as he watched in awe. Morgan and Raja had to drop to the ground and belly-crawl away from the truck. Young Arab men scrambled around on the parking lot cutting between parked semi-trucks on the lot, only to be cut off by heaving and huffing middle-aged overweight truck drivers with shotguns, baseball bats, and tire irons. The sky was ablaze with flashing red and blue lights. Sirens wailed, and tires screeched as police cars flocked into the parking lot. Floradixie, the largest truck stop in Florida, had become the biggest battleground in North America since the Civil War.

Our side won! We won!

As things settled down, would-be terrorists were found trembling in ditches and hiding beneath eighteen-wheelers. The lucky ones were face down, others dead or in various stages of dying. The state police kept a tight rein on the truckers, but they didn't reject their assistance. The terrorists were being pushed, shoved and jammed into paddy wagons by proud American combatants who shouted things like, "God bless America," and "Don't fuck with Uncle Sam!"

As the battle came to a halt, terrorists were

routed like scared rabbits from their holes. FBI and Homeland Security were arriving in droves. TV news trucks and camera crews descended onto the battlegrounds in a frenzied effort to capture the debacle on video. Ambulance crews and fire department personnel carried the wounded and the dead from the scene. A light rain settled in and saturated the ground. Rivulets of blood trickled into the truck ruts and pooled in the low spots on the parking lot. The tally was forty five dead, ten wounded and five had surrendered.

Morgan, Pedro, Raja and Rudy were identified as the offending agents in the milieu. They were apprehended and held in a storage room next to the truckers' lounge.

It was quiet outside except for an occasional exuberant outburst from the victors. There was blood in the streets, but the participants were as ecstatic as Choctaw fans after a Friday night thumping of the Ada Bulldogs. For most of them the reality had not yet set in. The blood and guts weren't ceremonial feathers and beads. The bodies weren't octopi on the ice at a hockey game.

The dead were the sons and fathers of someone, somewhere. Surely, when they came into the world kicking and screaming, their mothers didn't hope they would aspire to journey across the world to murder innocent people. Would their fathers be proud and happy as their sons lie face down on the asphalt riddled with lead? The world was truly in a deranged state of being, but common sense did still exist somewhere. It did, didn't it?

Killing someone should never be a pleasant experience. Movies, television, and books make it seem so, but taking someone's life without remorse isn't something ordinary people do.

The truckers, cycle riders, and motorists were celebrating at the moment, but when all was said and done, it would weigh heavy on them. They were all heroes. They had stepped up because they were citizens in the greatest country to occupy the earth. To defend her is an honor. But still at some point in the future they would all remember themselves chasing Arabs through the parking lot as though they were killing snakes. They were would-be murderers, but killing them was a duty having been done, not a competition for bragging rights.

There were armed guards standing at the door where Morgan, Rudy, Pedro and Raja were being held. They were handcuffed and seated in metal straight-back chairs, surrounded by canned vegetables and dry goods. There was a walk-in freezer humming in the corner. It wasn't exactly maximum security, but there was no danger they were going to flee.

Morgan knew that he had done things that the law wouldn't tolerate. The gunfight at the Majestic Hotel should have been reported. The law doesn't allow private citizens to take the law into their own hands.

They should have called the police to warn them about the pending attack on Hollywood Beach.

When he pulled the trigger on Yellow Eyes, he committed voluntary manslaughter.

There was a morass of conditions and circumstances that would mitigate their conduct, but in the end they had committed uncounted felonies and misdemeanors. If there was enough support from the public because of their heroism they might be able to negotiate for light sentences, but as sure as the world turns, they would be convicted of something. Morgan knew the system and there was no way out.

"Why didn't they ask for our names?" Rudy asked solemnly.

"My guess is the FBI wants to be the first to interview us," Morgan said.

"Do ya think they'll take us in, Morgan, down to the station house?"

"I don't know, Rudy."

"It don't seem fair. I mean, we stuck our necks out to save a bunch of innocent people, and now we're sitting here with our hands cuffed behind our backs." Rudy snorted.

"Rudy, we were cops. We know the law. We know how things are done. This was all outside the law, and we both knew it."

"We saved people. That's what I know. What bullshit!" Rudy shouted. After a few moments he lowered his eyebrows in thought and bit his lip. "I'm sorry about gett'n you into this mess. Morgan."

"Up until they put the irons on me, this was the best time I've had in three years. So don't blame yourself, we did it together. Besides that, what's wrong with saving the world?"

Just at that moment the door opened and a tall middle-aged man dressed in a gray pinstripe suit stepped through the doorway. He made eye contact with Morgan as he closed the door behind him. Morgan waited for him to introduce himself as Special Agent so-and-so, but he didn't. He was quiet as he studied the four captives. He strolled around the room casually as he inspected the surroundings.

After several moments he said, "Thank you for your service to our country."

"Are we in trouble?" Rudy asked.

"What do you think? he said quietly.

"Chin deep, I guess," Rudy said.

"I didn't see any identification," Morgan said.

"I'm Special Agent Kenneth Ford. Do you know why I'm here?" he asked.

"We're ex-cops. We know why you're here. You want us to tell you everything we know, and then you'll arrest us."

Agent Ford looked for a chair. Finding one he pulled up in front of Rudy and Morgan. He sat there quietly for a long time. It was customary to read Miranda Warnings, even when cops were being interrogated. Agent Ford didn't read the Miranda Warnings.

He started slowly. "You guys are from central Illinois. I'm familiar with Willoughby Hills, so we've got something in common. I was there several times when I was a kid. I grew up in Tazewell County."

"So you were born in Illinois?" Morgan said.

"No, Ohio - Columbus, but my parents were killed in a car accident, and my Grandpa raised me in Illinois. We lived on a farm out in Tazewell County. Grandpa used to take me with him to the farmer's elevator on Old Route 66 north of Willoughby Hills. We frequently went into town after we unloaded our corn, and we'd eat at Pop's Rocket Popcorn. We'd have corn dogs and fries with vinegar. Good stuff, man."

"We're not here to talk about corn dogs, are we, Agent Ford? Don't you want to know about terrorism and murder? And maybe you might want a confession from us, too." Morgan said.

Agent Ford ignored Morgan's remark. "My grandfather was the greatest man I ever knew. He was my hero in every way a man can be a hero. He fought in World War II. He met General Patton, and he knew Audie Murphy."

"The actor?" Rudy interrupted.

"The war hero. The most decorated soldier in American history – and yes, the actor. Grandpa was shot in North Africa, and then again in Italy, but he stayed in for the duration. After the war, he went back to Illinois and married my grandmother. She was a year older than Grandpa, but she waited for him faithfully until he came home. It's a clichéd tale but true. Grandpa scratched out a living on a one horse farm, but somehow he saved enough money to put me through school. His proudest moment was when I graduated from the FBI Academy and became an agent for the Bureau."

Morgan had seen interrogations conducted where the interviewer used conversation to break the ice – to warm up the person being interviewed, and then later he would go for the throat. He didn't get the sense that Agent Ford was going anywhere with this.

"Grandpa was a staunch Democrat in spite of how hard I tried to convert him. He loved John F. Kennedy. For forty years he wanted to go to Washington to visit Kennedy's grave, the Capitol and the White House."

Agent Ford got up from his chair and walked behind the four men. He reached into his pocket and retrieved a handcuff key. "He was just one old man, not really important in the whole scheme of things, but he was the most important man in the world to me."

He turned the key in Pedro's cuffs and the metal clicked open. Pedro rubbed his wrists to restore the blood.

"I sent him and his private healthcare provider to Washington D.C. for his 80th birthday. He was old and feeble but generally in pretty good health. I guess I should have gone with him, but I was busy with my career. His healthcare provider was only 24. I thought he was in good hands."

He opened the restraints on Rudy's arms, and left the key with him to open Morgan, and Raja's cuffs.

"He saw Kennedy's grave, the Washington Monument, the whole works. As a side bar they flew up to New York City to the World Trade Center – an afterthought, more or less."

Morgan, Rudy, Raja and Pedro were standing, watching Agent Ford as he walked to the back door of the storage room. Like sheep they followed him. Morgan was suddenly aware that Ford's grandfather was a victim of the 9/11 attack. Without knowing him, he admired Agent Ford. He admired all of those who were on the front lines fighting for the survival of the United States. Agent Ford was a career law enforcement official, and he was risking everything by being there. Morgan accepted that Anderson was on a quest for revenge, but he hadn't thought of Anderson as someone who was laying it on the line. Now he wondered if Anderson had been like Ford before he became a killer. He wasn't an FBI Agent. What horror had descended upon him to turn him into a killing machine? Who was taken from him? How deeply had he suffered? It made sense now. Anderson was a survivor, too.

Agent Ford opened the door. The red and blue lights from the emergency vehicles on the front parking lot where the battle had raged were still flashing. They glistened off the wet asphalt and light flickered inside the storage room.

Agent Ford stood holding the door open. "Like I said, gentlemen, thank you for your service to our country."

Silently they walked out the door. It was peculiar to walk away. Morgan thought he should be emotionally drained, but he wasn't. He didn't feel anything. He was numb. Morgan imagined there would have been a sense of accomplishment, or maybe fulfillment, something hot and burning. But, there was nothing but numbness. He was totally and completely numb.

Thelma was waiting there to pick them up.

Chapter Twenty Four

Thelma was quiet. She drove without being instructed as to where to go. She already knew their destination was the Sea Breeze Inn.

Morgan sat silently watching the dividing lines on the roadway coming and going beneath the headlight beams. Was Thelma sad? Was she grieving Anderson's death? Did she have a plan for tomorrow?

The sun was setting behind a line of palm trees in the west. The orange glow behind them was like a fire in the sky.

Morgan's emotional disconnect would erode with time, and he would have to confront his feelings. He knew in his heart he had done the right thing. There were soldiers decorated in every war who had done nothing more heroic than he and his companions. He, Rudy, and Pedro were involved in two battles, and God only knew the stress Raja had endured even before the first shot was fired. There would be no ceremonial congratulations for them.

It was their secret, but also their honor.

Morgan never wanted to kill anyone, but now he had. There was never any malice in his heart but being a decent man he would carry a burden.

It would manifest in regret for taking another man's life. He didn't have to feel sympathy for the men who died in the half-baked evil plan, but he needed to be numb to it. And so, he was.

Thelma stopped in front of the Sea Breeze Inn, like a cab driver delivering passengers to their destinations. As they were getting out Thelma called for Morgan. She handed him a folder. "Anderson wanted you to have this," she said.

Morgan took it and placed it under his arm. "What is it?" he asked.

"I don't know, but it was important to him." There was more than a hint of sadness in her eyes.

Morgan looked at her for a long time, and then he walked away. He and the other men went into the hotel lobby. Angelique, Sonya, Anna, and Maria were there. Maria ran to Pedro, sobbing and laughing at the same time. She threw her arms around him., clamoring in Spanish, and only she and Pedro knew what she said, but the sentiment was the same in any language. It was pure and simple relief. In spite of all the crap in his life, Pedro was a lucky man.

Morgan and Rudy were beat up and damaged. Sonya had used the lobby restroom to wash away some of Anderson's blood, but her clothes were still like a ring towel at the end of a 12-round boxing match.

The other women were completely and totally frazzled from the suspense and the waiting. Angelique had called for a friend to come for Jose, and he was recovering.

The miracle was that they were all alive.

After a few moments, Morgan signaled for the troop to accompany him to his room. The desk clerk watched them limp and struggle across the lobby with as much interest as a cocker spaniel watching golf on TV. He could see them, but he just wasn't interested. The Sea Breeze offered a daily dose of drama. Nothing shocked him anymore.

Once they were inside the room the men related their experiences to the women. Nobody asked questions. The melee was horrendous. Curiosity for detail was an element best left for another time, so Morgan was brief.

After the tale had been told, Morgan opened the folder Thelma had given him. He analyzed the contents for several moments in silence. The first item was a family picture of Anderson, his wife, and daughters. There was a yellow sticker attached to the photo. It said, "I am not a monster. My name is Anderson Claypool. I'm a husband, and father. I love my country. If you're reading this, then I am dead. Please keep the picture, and remember me, for now I have given everything."

Morgan's eyes welled with tears. He wasn't numb to that.

"What's wrong?" Rudy asked. At another time he would have asked if Morgan might have seen a beautiful woman's thighs, but he was devoid of humor at the moment.

"It's just something for me," he answered.

He opened several documents and examined each of them individually. What he found inside was astonishing. For Angelique, there was a copy of a Birth Certificate, and a note indicating that the original was on file at the County Courthouse in Wayne County, Arkansas.

The last Will and Testament of Harmon Edison was included, indicating that his entire fortune would go to

Sonya, and to Anna as Sonya's heir.

The next item was the hospital records of the live birth of Antonio Triano, including finger and footprints.

There was a copy of the Death Certificate of Rosa Triano, and her obituary in the San Francisco Chronicle indicating that she had no surviving heirs. A scribbled penciled note said, "You will have to do the rest yourself. DNA will stand up in court"

Lastly, there were two Green Cards for Pedro and Maria.

They all looked at the documents in total amazement. Morgan wondered if they were legitimate. Of course, they were. But how did Anderson find a way to make them real?

Angelique knew for sure that she didn't have a Birth Certificate, but she trusted what her eyes could see.

It wasn't likely that Harmon Edison had no inkling that he was going into the abyss ahead of schedule, so a Will and Testament leaving his money to Sonya was unlikely, but he did - or at least it appeared that he did.

All the documents were impossible to acquire, but still there they were, all in black and white.

Proving Jose's identity would be a can of corn, since his fingerprints were taken when he was born. The charges in Memphis would be no more than an annoyance with the money Jose would have to contest them.

It was all there in a neat little package. A folder full of miracles.

Pedro and Maria returned to the Majestic Hotel and went to their apartment as legal immigrants. They conducted a quick investigation to find that there were no dead bodies, bloody carpet, or bullet-riddled furniture on the twelfth floor. In fact, the walls were wearing a fresh coat of paint. There was a new manager on duty. He informed them that the owner had left for Saudi Arabia. It didn't matter to them because now that they were legal they were leaving for Galesburg, Illinois where they knew they could find work in a meat packaging plant. The green cards hadn't elevated their career ambitions, but it certainly gave them confidence to move about the country.

Morgan, Rudy, Angelique, Sonya and Anna all slept in Morgan's bed. It was a super king and provided wiggle room for them. They were packed together snugly, and for all they had been through the security of lying together was enough to offset the discomfort.

When morning came Sonya, Anna, and Angelique headed out. They said their goodbyes, but it wasn't the end of them. Each of them, including Pedro and Maria, would be friends until they parted in death.

Morgan and Rudy didn't leave. They caught up on their bill and went to the drugstore for pain relievers. They had breakfast at the local Cracker Barrel and read the newspapers.

The early reports on the conflict at Floradixie were that Homeland Security and the FBI had been involved in an ongoing investigation into terrorist activity for several weeks, culminating in the assault at the truck stop. They were praised by the Director of Homeland Security for the total cooperation between the agencies. According to unnamed sources, there were numerous agents on site monitoring the situation when the assault went down, and by their bravery and sacrifice hundreds of lives were saved. It was a good spin, and if nobody came up with a better scenario it would probably work.

The maid service at the Sea Breeze wasn't exactly exemplary, so Morgan went back to his room and cleaned it thoroughly. He trimmed his hair and took a shower. He needed a distraction. He continually relived the previous day in his mind moment by moment. It helped to stay busy. When he had finished he walked down to Rudy's room. Rudy was sitting on the bed wearing his black Memphis Zoo polo shirt and tan swimming trunks.

Without speaking Rudy got up and clicked off the TV set. Morgan grabbed the beach chairs, and they went down the hallway, out the broken emergency exit doorway, and out onto the beach.

It was late in the afternoon and dark clouds had gathered out on the ocean. A gray curtain of rain was visible on the horizon. It was clear in the west and as blue as an indigo sky on a Colorado mountaintop. The sea had turned dark green; high tide was churning the waves and oblique rays from the setting sun were striking the white caps and emblazoned them in an amber haze as they marched row upon row onto the beach.

It was peaceful in spite of all the chaos and insanity. It was as though nothing had happened. A circle of "Knucks" in beach chairs talked loudly in French and participated in the international language of laughter and song.

Neither Morgan nor Rudy understood a word but they smiled as they watched.

Finally Morgan spoke, "What are we gonna do now, Rudy?"

Rudy looked out into the ocean as he was given

to do. "Maybe we could cash in our annuities, borrow a couple million and buy the Sea Breeze and fix 'er up."

"It'll take more than two million," Morgan said.

"Four million, then."

"I thought maybe we could go home," Morgan said.

Rudy didn't answer. There was no answer necessary. It was all there was left to do. They remained on the beach until after the sun sunk beneath the horizon.

When morning came they were packed and northbound on I-95.

Chapter Twenty Five

It was December. There had been a snowfall during the night. It wasn't enough to cancel school, create traffic nightmares, or cause people to hole up in their homes. It was just enough to remind Illinoisans that winter was upon them. Illinois is desolate during the winter months. The ground is frozen, trees are barren, and the sky is cloaked in a dreary gray. Only the sturdy or those trapped in tradition would prefer the cold sting of a brisk prairie wind to palm trees and a gentle ocean breeze.

Morgan was born in Willoughby Hills, and he was a traditionalist, but since he had returned home his mind was still rambling around in Hollywood, Florida. Maybe he would become a snowbird and migrate south during the winter. The prospect was appealing but he wasn't going to think about it right then. At the moment he was off to Freda's to meet Rudy for coffee. They were falling back into their old routines.

When Morgan went to the garage he was surprised to find it was jammed packed with boxes full of exercise equipment. He searched for the manifest ticket but found nothing. It was a safe bet that the delivery truck had found its way to the wrong address. It wasn't something he could ignore, but it could wait until after he had his morning coffee.

As he made his way to Freda's, the feather-light snow danced along on the wind and floated away from the windshield as if it had a mind not to be impeded. The parking spaces in front of the restaurant were full. Every farmer and anyone else not working due to the weather was uptown drinking coffee and chewing the fat about the underwear bomber, or the socialists take-over of the healthcare system.   It was a recent phenomenon that people thought they could change the world by simply talking about it.

The bell jingled over the door as Morgan stepped inside. The smell of bacon grease permeated the air, and spoons rattled in cups as the crowded room clinked, stirred and clamored. The booth where the cops usually sat was empty. Freda's had been the local favorite for the various police agencies for fifty years. They always sat in the same place. No regular customer would occupy that space for fear they might be funding the court coffers for their trespass. It was like having a seat on reserve at all times.

Curtis Hardy, a local state police officer was paying his tab at the register as Morgan made his way to the booth. "Hey, Morg, what's happening, Old Henry?" Curtis said. He had been calling Morgan Old Henry for 20 years. According to Curtis, Morgan had a physical resemblance to Henry Cambridge, a Jewel Tea and Coffee man who delivered his goods to customers in Morgan's neighborhood. It had started as an "Ah, yo momma," type joke, but Curtis wouldn't give it up.

Morgan took a seat and Curtis came back to the booth. "How's it going, Curtis?"

"Good, I've got eight tickets already this morning," he said proudly, fanning the tickets with his thumb.

Morgan smiled. He was never impressed with traffic enforcement. Now that he had gone to the mat with the most dangerous element in the annals of crime he was even less interested. It was his secret though, his and Rudy's. He couldn't put it on display like so many tickets fanning in the air.

"How's retirement, Morg?" Curtis asked.

"It's okay. I've been staying busy serving papers."

"Do you ever miss real police work? I know you local guys didn't get in on all that much, but the Saturday night fights and all. You gotta miss break'n up them fights." He stroked the brim of his Smoky hat.

Morgan believed the state police were little more than traffic wardens, but he didn't contest the back-door insult. Morgan had seen more "real police work" on the road to Floradixie than Curtis had seen in twenty five years, but it didn't matter.

Rudy came into the restaurant to a smattering of "Hey Rudy's" from coffee customers from all over the room. He was like Norm on Cheers. As he plopped into the booth he said, "Hey, Hot Air, how's it going?" Curtis and Rudy didn't know how to talk without bantering.

"I'd say, but you wouldn't be able to hear me."

"You'd be wrong, Dudley Do-Right. I was in Memphis a while back and I bought a Miracle Ear. I hear it all now, boy."

"Right," Curtis said.

"No really, I just heard someone all the way across the room whisper, hey, see that big fat state trooper over there standing around wasting our tax dollars."

Morgan had noticed that Rudy's hearing had improved, but he hadn't said anything about it. He noticed the loud talking had toned down a little, too.

Rudy squirmed in his chair. " I need to talk to you," his whispered. He was like a man with an itch in his ear at a formal dinner table. He needed to get at it, but he had to wait for an opportune moment. He rolled his eyes as Curtis ignored the remark and started talking about speeders and expired license plates.

Rudy interrupted. "Hey, Curtis, there's innocent unsuspecting motorists out on I-55 you can bag for $75.00 a pop!" he said.

"I can take a hint, I'm going, but speeding ain't no innocent activity," Curtis said as he headed for the door.

Rudy waited until Curtis was gone, but he was busting at the seams to spill something. Rudy couldn't handle a mystery. He was one of those people who took things apart to see the interior workings and was never able to put them back together. He was the same about anything suspicious. Something unusual had happened to him before he left for the restaurant, and he was bent on getting input from Morgan.

"Morgan, something really strange happened to me this morning. I went into my basement and there was a whole bunch of exercise equipment down there that I didn't buy. My doors were locked so I don't know how somebody could have got in there, but it was crammed with boxes of stuff. There was a year's supply of diet food, and a weekly menu and some workout instructions. I either lost my mind and bought a bunch of crap and forgot about it, or a ghost found its way into my basement."

Morgan analyzed the situation. "That is strange. I had some exercise equipment left in my garage. It has to be more than coincidence."

Just at that moment a young man was standing at the doorway studying them. Morgan was first to notice him. "Rudy, who is that guy looking at us?" he asked. Rudy looked and saw a man in a gray suit, with a freshly cropped hair cut. He was slender and well-groomed. His face was familiar, but Rudy was stumped.

In an instant, Morgan grinned. "It's The Jesus – our Messiah impersonator, all dressed up."

Based on their past experiences with him, Morgan thought he might take off in a cloud of dust. He was quick in sandals, Morgan doubted they would stand a chance against him in real shoes. The man walked slowly across the room. He was carrying an envelope in his hand. He stopped at the booth and slid the envelope across the table. He turned and smiled over his shoulder as he walked away. It wouldn't have surprised Morgan if he had faded into a miasma and disappeared.

Morgan picked up the envelope and stared at it for a long time. Finally he opened it.

It read, "Get in shape. You've been drafted."

The End

CPSIA information can be obtained
at www.ICGtesting.com
Printed in the USA
LVHW041728290820
664471LV00009B/1071